JAPANESE ROBOTS
LOVE TO DANCE

Margret A. Treiber

Azoth Khem Publishing
Huntsville, AL
January 2025

AZOTH KHEM

ISBN: 978-1-952880-19-3
First Edition 2018
Second Edition 2023
Third Edition 2024

Azoth Khem Publishing
29931 Copperpenny Drive NW
Harvest, AL 35749
www.azothkhem.com

Ordering Information:
Quantity sales and exclusive discounts are available on quantity
purchases by corporations, associations, and others. For details,
contact the publisher at the address above. For orders by U.S. trade
bookstores and wholesalers, please contact
Azoth Khem Publishing: Tel: (256) 221-5498 or visit
www.azothkhem.com

Printed in the United States of America

Dedication

To Laura and Elliot Treiber, whom I miss a great deal. I wish you would have been alive to read this.

Thank you to Jennifer McGuire for fixing this manuscript.

Thanks to my critique group, Joyce and Christopher, for making it not suck enough to hand it over to Jen.

And thank you to my wife Marie-Jessique, who rarely gets the accolades she deserves.

Contents

.

Part 1
Gary Legal, Attorney at Law

"Just because two people can wreak glorious destruction together, it doesn't mean they should date," Gabe Siegel stated matter-of-factly. "This is the third time this year."

"I know, I know," replied the young man from across the cluttered desk. "You don't know her. I try to stay away, but she's like a magnet, you know? We get pulled together and—boom!"

"Yes, I know. Boom, property damage. Expensive, record-generating demolition. You need to actively avoid her. If you see her coming, you go the other way."

"I'm addicted. I try to stay away, but I can't. I didn't know she was trouble, I wouldn't have hooked up with her."

"Didn't know? The fact that she's a member of the Sisterhood of the Immaculate Vengeance wasn't a hint?"

The young man shrugged. "I thought it was a band."

Gabe shook his head. "Joe, leave her alone. Here's a plan: Go to work, go home. Don't go out. Don't date. Just watch porn and play video games. Hell, I'll buy you

1

a game console and talk to your probation officer. But you have to stay clean for the next eighteen months."

"I don't have a job," Joe replied. "I lost it when the mall blew up."

Gabe clutched his temples. "You're killing me, man. Okay, I'll talk to some people. Can you stay clean?"

Joe nodded. "Yup, I promise. Thank you, Mr. Siegel."

Gabe winced. "Gabe. Call me Gabe. Mr. Siegel is my dad."

"Isn't your dad that political douche with all the vid ads?"

Gabe grimaced. "Yeah, my dad is running for office."

"So why aren't you all in there with his posse, living the life?"

"I don't get along too well with them. They're a bunch of creeps only interested in lining their pockets. I'm more of an everyday guy kind of lawyer."

"But you got money, right? I mean, look at that watch. That's a Cartier, right?"

"It belonged to my grandfather," Gabe replied. "My mother gave it to me. How do you know about watches?"

"My mother worked at Tay's Jewelry when I was a kid."

2

"You're still a kid."

"You're still a rich boy."

"Touché," Gabe replied.

"So why do you work this lousy legal aid job? Couldn't you get a better one? Did you piss someone off?"

Gabe grinned. "I had plenty of offers. Folks were only pissed off after I took this gig. Some still think I did it to aggravate my dad."

"Did you?" Joe asked.

Gabe shrugged. "Maybe it was part of the reason."

Joe laughed. "Respect, Mister…I mean, Gabe. You should ditch the watch, though. It stands out. And maybe get a new suit. You look like a Guy's Warehouse ad. Nobody will trust you."

"Is that all?" Gabe asked. "How's my hair? Too short?"

"Hair's okay, but your name…Gabe is so…"

"So what?"

"So…dweeb. You should try something different, like Greg or Garth or something."

"Garth?" Gabe replied. "No, I'm not changing my name."

"Just saying."

"I'll consider your other advice." Gabe stood up and shook Joe's hand. "I'll call you in a couple of days about a job, okay?"

Joe returned Gabe's handshake. "Okay."

Joe left the building, looking relieved, as if a weight had been lifted. Gabe made notes on his desktab, nearly finished when he heard a loud screech followed by a crash outside. He glanced out the window to see a woman beating a caddibot. She kicked it repeatedly, berating it with curse words and insults. Gabe could almost swear the bot was cowering. It squeaked in distress as she struck it again, trying to spin its round, scuffed-up body out of reach, wobbling from the weight of its basket. Gabe jumped up and ran out into the street.

"Hey, lady," he yelled. "You can't just beat that thing like that."

"And who are you, the robot defense league?" The woman glared at Gabe. "This thing won't even roll. What do you want me to do with it?"

"I don't know," Gabe replied. "Maybe fix it. Look, it's not rolling because it probably hasn't been lubricated in months. Can't you hear the thing screaming?"

"Screaming?" she scoffed. "It's a cart. It doesn't scream." She kicked the bot again. It squealed.

"What the hell is that? Don't you hear that?"

"If you want it to save it so bad, fifty coins, and it's yours."

Gabe reached into his pocket and pulled out fifty cashcoins.

"Here." He shoved the coins into her hand, "You heartless crone."

Gabe scooped up the caddibot and brought it inside.

"Don't worry, little fella," Gabe said. "After work, we'll find a repair shop for you."

The caddibot chirped.

Gabe settled the caddibot in a padded box on the floor next to his desk. The caddibot went into power-saving mode while Gabe worked on the remainder of his cases.

"Hey, Gabe." Gabe's supervisor, Dora, stepped into his cubicle.

"Howdy, Dora," Gabe replied, looking up from his case files.

"I heard you stuck your neck out for Joe again."

"Yeah," Gabe answered. "He's a good kid. He just made some poor choices."

"Be careful," Dora warned him. "Word is getting out that you're using Daddy's connections to spring your clients."

"That's not true," Gabe objected. "I know these people on my own. Dad's connections hate me."

"Whatever the truth is, rumors are rumors, and they are getting around. Tell your clients to stop blabbing."

"I'll do my best."

"Good. What's with the caddibot?"

"Oh, him?" Gabe motioned at the robot. "Project. Gonna get him fixed up."

"It looks like it's seen better days. The ServiceBot people will be by this week if you want them to take care of it. They can swap it out for a refurb."

Gabe shook his head. "Nah, it's my personal bot. I'll take care of it."

"Whatever." Dora rolled her eyes. "You're a strange camper. I'll be in meetings for the rest of the day, so I'll see you tomorrow."

"Okay." Gabe nodded and returned to his files.

The rest of the day was uneventful. Gabe worked with an assortment of clients, all defendants in criminal cases, all in need of friendly advice and a simple break more than the actual legal aid they came in for. Gabe found it draining but far more satisfying than he'd anticipated when he'd accepted the position.

At the end of the day, he collected the caddibot and headed over to the shops. He knew he'd find an eager vendor willing to void a warranty for the right coin.

Elmo's Electronic Emporium was fairly busy. Gabe walked in and immediately noticed the slobby man standing behind the counter. He was engaged in a debate with a customer over the proper uses for a Wafflizer. He paused his animated discussion when Gabe stepped forward and placed the caddibot on the counter.

"What's that?" the slobby man asked.

"It's my caddibot," Gabe replied. "It needs repair."

"So, send it to the manufacturer. They'll send you a refurb."

"But I want to fix this one," Gabe replied.

"Why?" the slobby man asked. "Nobody fixes 'em anymore. They recycle them. Bring it back for a credit; get a new one. Look how banged up it is. Stop being cheap."

"It's not about being cheap," Gabe stated. "I have a certain attachment to this little bot."

The slobby man scowled at Gabe. "What? Are you some kind of weirdo?"

"You know what? Never mind." Gabe grabbed the caddibot off the counter. "I'll take it someplace else."

"Good luck with that," the slobby man shouted. "It's illegal to tamper with it. It's in the user agreement."

Gabe waved his hand in dismissal and stormed out the door.

The next shop was Annie's Automatics. It was quiet and empty. An elderly lady sat in a chair watching game shows on her vid monitor. She stood up when she saw Gabe walk in.

"How can I help you?" she asked.

"Good afternoon, ma'am," Gabe replied. "I'm here to get my caddibot repaired."

"Oh my," the woman said. "It's seen a great deal of use."

"Yes," Gabe stated. "I got this little fella from a friend, and I want to fix him up."

"Did they transfer the license to you?"

"Well, no. They just gave him to me."

"They can't do that," she pointed out. "They have to give you the license. It's in the user agreement."

"But we can fix it, right? I'll get the license from my friend later."

"No." The lady shook her head. "Once you get the license, you go to the manufacturer, and they replace it. It's illegal to tamper with the components. It's in—

"—the user agreement. I got it."

Gabe left the shop, clutching the caddibot. It gazed at him, its electronic eyes almost registering fear. Gabe shook his head, trying to dismiss the sensation. It was a machine. It couldn't be afraid.

But no matter how hard he rationalized it, Gabe could not escape a feeling of pity for this thing.

He had one last idea. He would hit the underground market. It sat below street level, under the entire block. It was almost like a flea market—a gray zone, housing shops that sold everything from cheap trinkets to black-market goods. Gabe knew that someone inside would be willing to help him with the right amount of coin.

He got to the entrance and was greeted by a posse of armed young men.

"What you want?" one of the young men asked.

"I'm here to do business," Gabe replied. "Like everyone else."

"You can afford to go above ground."

"Yeah," Gabe smirked. "You know how it is. Some stuff is hard to find, some places."

The man studied Gabe hard. "Aren't you the guy who helped Bobo with the snack thing?"

Gabe nodded. "I remember that. Wrong change."

"Yeah." The man pointed at Gabe. "This is the guy who got Bobo cut loose."

The others mumbled and parted, revealing free access to the door.

"Thanks, guys." Gabe walked by, waving at them as he stepped inside.

The place was alive. Gabe liked the humanity of it. It wasn't the sterile, ostentatious environment he grew up in. These were real people; organic, sloppy, and living. Gabe breathed it in.

"Re, re!" A man tugged on the sleeve of Gabe's shirt. "You need some pharmaceuticals? You got pain, stomach acid, allergies?"

Gabe shook his head. "No, but I need medical attention for this guy." Gabe motioned at the caddibot.

"Why don't you just trade that thing in? The company will give you a new one."

"Eh," Gabe replied. "I'd rather just fix this one."

"Ha! You have feelings for that thing?" The man laughed. "Hey, Po!" he shouted to a man seated on a stool in a sunglass booth. "This guy is like your wife with the vac."

Po laughed and pointed at Gabe. "Did you name it?"

"No," Gabe replied. "No, I did not."

"Not yet," the first man stated. "Give it time."

"Oh, come on," Gabe whined. "Look at it. It's got a face. How am I supposed to feel?"

The two men laughed. "Go down the way and find Ji-hoon," Po said. "He'll help you."

Gabe nodded. "Thanks."

"You take care of your little friend." The two men continued to cackle. Gabe was meters away before their laughter faded into the crowd.

It took a few more inquiries before Gabe found Ji-hoon's booth. Ji-hoon was a small Asian man on the older side of middle-aged. His smile was warm, and his demeanor was inviting.

"How may I help you?" he asked.

"The drug pusher and the sunglass guy said you may be able to help me fix my caddibot. And before you start,

I don't want to trade him in for a new one and I don't have the license. I want to fix this one."

"Why?" Ji-hoon asked.

"Listen, I know it's just a thing. I get it. But this woman was beating the crap out of it outside my office. Nothing deserves to be treated like that, even a robot that everybody's so eager to throw away."

"So you feel sorry for it."

"Yeah," Gabe admitted. "I guess I do. What is so wrong with that?"

"Not a damned thing," Ji-hoon replied. "I'll see what I can do."

"You're not afraid of copyrights or voiding warranties?"

Ji-hoon laughed. "No. I'm a little past that."

"What does that mean?" Gabe asked.

Ji-hoon shook his head. "That means that's the least of my concerns. Me and the law have bigger fish to fry than a voided home appliance warranty. Is that a problem?"

"No," Gabe replied. "No problem at all."

"Good. Let me take a look at this fellow. Come on in."

Gabe followed Ji-hoon into his booth. The booth had a workbench and some shelves with parts stacked on them. There was a curtain in the back that appeared to hide some kind of stock area. Gabe handed the caddibot to Ji-hoon, who carefully placed the bot on the bench and pulled out some electronic tools. He probed and tested for some time before he put his tools down.

"You definitely got this secondhand," Ji-hoon stated.

"Yeah, I liberated him from that witch with the loose right foot."

Ji-hoon nodded. "You don't look like the type to withhold lubrication from a machine. This robot was deliberately abused."

"Can you fix it?"

Ji-hoon nodded tentatively. "Technically, yes. I can replace the broken motors, but these bots were designed to fail in the event of tampering. It's possible that after I repair it, it could still experience a cascading failure. I'll try to work around it."

"What are the chances?"

"Good," Ji-hoon replied. "I'm an electrical engineer."

A gravelly laugh resonated from behind the curtain.

"Is someone back there?"

"Just my grandson," Ji-hoon loudly announced. "Ignore him. He has no manners."

"Hokay," Gabe replied. "When can you start the repairs, and how much do I owe you?"

Ji-hoon shrugged. "I'll start now. Honestly, the parts are barely a quarter coin. I'll do it for free. This way, if we are questioned, I was just doing a favor for a friend."

"That's really nice of you," Gabe replied. "Why would you do something like that?"

"I have a weakness for downtrodden robots, I guess."

A grunt emanated from the back.

"Silence!" Ji-hoon threw a screwdriver at the curtain.

"Well, if you ever need a favor, let me know. Here's my card." Gabe handed Ji-hoon his personal card with his private comm number.

"You're an attorney?"

"Yup," Gabe answered. "I work for the community legal center. But we could work something out."

Ji-hoon grinned. "You're going to hear back from us soon."

"Us? Should I be afraid?"

"Probably," Ji-hoon admitted.

"Cool, thanks for the warning."

"It's going to take a while to fix this. I can have it ready in the morning."

14

"Perfect," Gabe replied. "I'll bring coffee, or are you a tea guy?"

"Tea, please."

"You got it. See you in the a.m."

The next morning, Gabe arrived at Ji-hoon's booth, tea in hand. Ji-hoon was waiting with a smile on his face.

"Here you go, my friend." Gabe handed Ji-hoon the tea.

Ji-hoon bowed his head and accepted the tea. "Thank you."

"It's nothing. How's the little robot?"

"Fine, all fixed up. I left the dents because I think they give him character. He has a new coat of paint. I replaced two motors and serviced all the components. Just keep him lubricated, and he'll be fine."

"Excellent! Sure, I don't owe you anything?"

"I'll take it out as a favor one day." Ji-hoon extended his hand.

"You've piqued my curiosity." Gabe took Ji-hoon's hand and shook it. "I look forward to it. Come on, caddibot. Let's go home."

"Oh, yeah," Ji-hoon said. "It's probably obvious, but don't bring it in for service. They'll destroy him, and we'll get busted for contract violation."

"Gotcha. Only bring him here."

Gabe left the market and made his way to the office. Caddibot chirped a cheerful song as he carried Gabe's briefcase down the sidewalk. The day just seemed that much brighter with the little robot's perky presence.

When they arrived, Dora was waiting.

"What's up?" Gabe asked. "Did I miss a staff meeting?"

"No," she replied. "Your boy Joe is back in jail. He and his girl trashed a BuyMart last night."

"Great. And I was having such a good morning."

"It gets worse. They want your head. Word is out that you have been back-dealing on behalf of your clients."

"Everybody does it. So what?"

"Not poor folk. This isn't going to go well for you."

"Wonderful." Gabe looked at the ground. "Maybe it's time to go into private practice."

"Just be humble. Let them reprimand you. Promise whatever they ask. They're waiting. Are you ready?"

"Yeah, let's go." Gabe turned to the caddibot. "Hang out here, lay low. Recharge or something."

The bot chirped a response and quickly plugged into an outlet under Gabe's desk.

Dora and Gabe walked into the conference room and were immediately besieged. Senior staff and some county officials sat, prepared with case notes and angry frowns. Gabe took a deep breath and stepped forward.

They all stared at him in silence until a representative from the county spoke.

"You've managed to piss just about everyone off. Your father is not going to save your ass this time. What do you have to say for yourself?"

"I was only trying to help my clients."

"You mean like Joe Jones? He's a real winner, a pillar of the community. And he isn't even the worst one. I have a list here of trash you pushed through the system using your connections. It's not—"

There was a knock on the door. One of the staff opened it, and a technician from ServiceBot stepped inside.

"This is a private meeting," Dora said. "What can we do for you?"

"Who owns the illegal caddibot out there?" the technician asked.

"We don't have any illegal bots here. What are you talking about?"

"The caddibot with the illegal modifications out there. You would think a law center would understand the consequences of breaking a user contract. We will be reporting this. Be prepared for an audit."

Gabe clutched his temples. "It was me. I take full responsibility. Where is my robot? I'll get him out of here."

"You want your robot? Here. Hey, Frank," the tech yelled out the door. "Hand me the hackbot."

He reached through the door and pulled in a trash bag. Gabe gasped as the technician dumped the contents of the bag at Gabe's feet. The pieces of caddibot tumbled into a pathetic pile.

"Deactivated," the technician continued. "That's what happens to illegal robots. And you will not be getting a replacement. Your warranty is void."

Gabe said nothing. He threw the parts back in the bag and took it with him as he walked out of the room. A moment later, Dora followed.

"Gabe, I'm sorry…"

"I only knew him a short time, but he was a great bot. He didn't deserve to suffer like that."

"Bot?" Dora scoffed. "I'm not talking about the robot. I'm talking about your job, your career. You're out. And your reputation? You won't be able to practice law once they're through with you. Now everyone will know that Gabe Siegel is the bleeding-heart, contract-breaking idiot who threw his career away on scumbag clients and broken robots. Do you know what you've done?"

Gabe shook his head and put his hand on Dora's shoulder. "It's okay."

"It's not okay. You're the laughingstock of the legal community."

"Yeah, but not to the people that count." Gabe grabbed his briefcase and his dead robot and shuffled out of the law center.

"So, you took my advice and changed your name," Joe said as he sat across the desk.

"Well, you didn't give me much of a choice. I was almost disbarred because of you."

"I thought it was because of the robot."

"The robot was just the icing on the cake."

"Sorry," Joe muttered. "But I like Gary Legal. It's a lot better than Gabe Siegel. Less political."

"You mean less like my dad." Gary shrugged. "I like it, too. It's campy and low-brow."

"It's perfect."

Gary nodded. "It is. So, tell me about your most recent dealings with the Sisterhood of the Immaculate Vengeance."

"Mr. Legal!" the receptionist, Denise, yelled across the office.

Gary held up his comm's receiver. "Intercom, Denise. Use it."

The intercom buzzed. "Mr. Legal?"

"Yes, Denise."

"Mr. Ji-hoon is on the comm for you. He says it's about that case you talked about."

Part 2
Body Building 101
0

I regarded the actuator with some scrutiny. "It's seen significant use."

"No, no, no, no, no," the junk merchant said. "Is good. Good stuff."

"Not a quarter coin good," I replied. "Maybe a point zero-seven coin good."

The infotainment system in the back of the shop cascaded streams of useless data about celebrities and impending economic calamity. The feed was peppered with advertisements for flying cars, insurance policies, and accident attorneys. The sound of it blended with the drone of the voices that filled the store, combining it into a cacophony of disharmony that sang the agony of humanity. The tune would crescendo and then fall to a barely audible murmur, but it was always there. It saturated the city with its dark, sticky suffering. Still within this hymn to humanity's suffering lay a descent melody barely audible: hope. Listening to that melody made the rest of the song bearable.

A weary-looking woman pushed a stroller into the shop, navigating through the narrow corridor between the counter and the piles of boxes and crates. She picked a dusty picture frame from a plastic bin and examined it. The child in the stroller squirmed and complained about her confinement. I experienced a momentary twinge of sympathy for the child, but it passed when she started whining excessively.

"Point eighteen coin good," the man counter offered.

The little girl in the stroller went from complaining to crying. Her mother tried to calm her by rolling the stroller back and forth. She was so preoccupied with the picture frame that she didn't notice my leg as she slammed the stroller into it. I barely felt it, so I didn't respond. The little girl, however, took one look at my bulk and screeched at full volume. Protocol dictated that I should say something comforting to the child, but it would not have helped.

"The likelihood of failure within the year is forty-eight percent. That decreases the value significantly." I continued to haggle, satisfying the shopkeeper's expectations. "An eighth coin, and that's my final offer."

"Point fifteen, how about point fifteen?" The man tried to look into my eyes but saw only his own reflection in the lenses of my sunglasses. Behind me, the mother scurried off, pushing her screaming offspring out of the store.

"Okay." The shop owner threw up his arms. "You win. An eighth coin, you filthy bastard."

"Thank you." I transferred the coin to the vendor's account and put the actuator in my coat pocket, safe and sound.

"Choke on it, bastard," he said.

"I require a physical receipt, please," I replied.

The man grumbled as he punched the keys on his antiquated register. A piece of paper advanced from the feed, and the shop owner tore it off begrudgingly. I took it from his extended arm, and he snarled at me. The man shuffled off to another potential customer, who was rummaging through a box of broken kitchen appliances.

I was not likely to return to this shop. The part was substandard and significantly overpriced. However, I only needed something to last me the short amount of time it would take to locate a superior replacement. I walked out onto the busy city street. The morning was bright and cool. The sun illuminated the many shades of gray that marked the centuries of repair on these utilitarian, twenty-first-century buildings. A spiced peanut vendor skillfully coordinated sales and food preparation for a crowd of hungry customers. I enjoyed witnessing the satisfied expressions of the patrons as they ate.

"Re, re, re, Al, namst!" Boy, a young man of sixteen, bounded over with seemingly boundless exuberance. He was approximately one-point-eight meters tall, thin but healthy-looking, and was wearing a baseball cap and oversized clothing. He looked like a child who had raided his older brother's wardrobe, which was the latest fashion.

"G-pop just got your stuff. He sent me to relay."

"Will he be conducting business this evening?"

"Yeah." Boy snorted. "You gonna take a bath sometime this year?" He waved his hand in front of his face, wincing.

"I maintain nominal hygiene."

"Not. You smell like a bum. When you gonna replace that raggedy coat?"

I quickly assessed the condition of my raincoat. "The coat is intact."

"It's old and busted, like that nasty hat and corroded scarf."

"They function as designed," I stated.

"They should function in the trash, man," Boy said. "That thing's full of stains. Score one tonight at the market."

"I will consider it if I have the coin."

"You're a strange, freaky tapori."

His focus went from me to a young woman across the street who was standing with a group of unwholesome-looking young men. "Re, Kami!" he yelled. "Gotta go." He ran over to the girl.

I recalled Boy's grandfather stating that Boy lacked an attention span. His behavior served to validate that supposition.

I examined my jacket again. Although Boy was correct in his assertion that it was stained, it served its main purpose. It covered. I would consider his suggestion; however, I would not likely make a change unless the attire failed its primary use.

I continued to the dipu. It was a short distance, so I arrived within a few minutes. Typically, the jobs were filled by early morning. However, despite it being late morning, I made it in time to catch one of the last remaining jobs. A dull buzz filled the work center as men of all ages talked and partook in the complimentary tea and cookies the center provided. For some, this would be the only meal they would have all day. I took a cup and filled it a quarter of the way, holding it as I navigated the facility. The crowd waiting for work was small. Most of the men who had not gotten jobs earlier had already left. There were about a dozen of us waiting when a work vehicle pulled up.

We queued up by the vehicle and one by one, men climbed into the vehicle bed as the foreman checked off boxes on his pad and confirmed that each worker had a valid wallet. I got in line behind a tired-looking man. He dragged himself up into the bed and sat on an empty, inverted bucket.

"You." The foreman pointed at me. "Why are you all covered up? Are you sick or something? The boss only wants men who can pull their weight."

"I'm fine," I answered. "I'm strong."

"Yeah, prove it." the foreman said. "Show me your face."

"Here."

I lifted the back of the work vehicle with my right arm. The man on the bucket fell down as it shifted upward. "I am strong." I put the vehicle back down on the ground.

"You on drugs, boy?" the foreman asked.

"No, reinforced arm. Army rebuild." It was a believable lie. "They didn't rebuild my face so well."

"You have a wallet?" he asked.

"Yes," I answered, "I do."

"Good." The foreman nodded. "Okay, get in."

I jumped in and sat on the floor of the vehicle bed. Nobody even gave me a second glance. We just drove in silence until we pulled into a construction site.

The site was mostly a pile of rubble. It was surrounded on all sides by standing, occupied buildings, so bringing large, heavy machinery on-site was a problem. They needed brute force to clear the lot. My job was loading debris into a wheelbarrow and emptying it into a dumpster. The labor was satisfactory and calming. I was able to focus on a single task without having to balance too many other parameters and contingencies in my mind. It was straightforward and goal-oriented work, which was just the kind of task I was most familiar with.

"Okay, everyone," the foreman called. "Break time."

The men all gathered by a food vehicle, standing around, conversing, and eating. I purchased a drink and a desi sandwich.

One of the men waved me over.

"Be right back," I said. "Need to call the girlfriend."

I walked around the corner and found a homeless man leaning against a wall.

"Hungry?" I asked, offering him the drink and sandwich.

"Yeah," he said. "Aren't you?"

"No," I replied. "I won't be able to eat this before it spoils."

"Thanks." He took the food, unwrapping the sandwich with enthusiasm.

"Here," I held out my hand. "I'll take the trash. I'm passing the can on my way back."

The man shrugged and handed me the sandwich wrapper.

"Thank you." I took the wrapper and headed back to the sight. When I was by the food vehicle, I threw the wrapper in the trash, making sure I was noticed. I made it back before the men finished their lunches and remained among them until they dispersed. I made my way back to my work area and continued where I left off. I cleared out my assigned area plus an extra ten square feet.

As we were climbing into the work vehicle to be dropped off at the dipu, the foreman approached me. "I noticed you. You keep to yourself, and you're a good worker. I like that."

"Thank you," I replied.

He held out his hand. "Name is Jackson."

I shook his hand. "Al."

"Nice to meet you, Al. You wouldn't happen to be interested in more work?"

"Yes, I would be interested."

"Good," he said. "I'll put you on my crews from now on. Just keep showing up. Six o'clock, Monday through Saturday. Sound good?"

"Yes," I replied. "That sounds good."

"Excellent!" Jackson smacked me on the shoulder. "I'll see you in the morning."

The vehicle drove us back to the dipu. I was paid two and a half coins. The payment was much higher than I expected for a day's work.

My home was a single-room apartment in a downtrodden part of the city. Although the populace was poor, there was less crime than might be expected. This was the kind of neighborhood where people were too concerned about caring for their families to risk prison time. I was steps from the door when I was abruptly stopped.

"Mr. Al, Mr. Al." A middle-aged, haggard woman approached me with a waiflike, preteen girl in tow. "Mr. Al, I am so sorry to bother you."

"You are not bothering me," I assured her.

"It's just that Mrs. Rodriguez told me that you may be able to help us." She looked around to make sure the street was clear. "I know she wasn't supposed to tell, but it is urgent. Bea got into the honors program on scholarship, but it doesn't cover books. I can get them all for free, but they are on paynet."

"The paynet is expensive. That is not free. Do you have a list of the books?"

"Yes." She nodded. "Here." She handed me a list of textbooks and the website to obtain them.

"Okay, this will take a moment." I pulled out a lappad, which I used as a prop to conceal my direct access to the nets. I connected to the paynet, using one of my backdoors, and connected to the site. The mistake most people make is downloading everything they see. That triggers site security and alerts the administrators. Mimicking normal use is the key, like a parent getting their child's schoolbooks. That is exactly what I did. I downloaded only the textbooks on the list. I saved a copy of the books on a spare, clear drive. I pulled the writer out of my pocket so the little girl could see the flashing and sparkling of lasers through the diamonds as it wrote the data. Her face lit up, as it did with most children witnessing the process.

"Here," I said when the process was complete and held out the drive to the equally excited mother.

She took the drive and reached into her pocket. "How much?

"No, no charge," I said. "Just help your daughter do well in school, and don't tell anyone where you got it."

Her smile overtook her face. "Thank you, thank you."

"You are welcome."

Her movement virtually evolved into a dance as she guided the girl into the building.

I arrived home and took twenty-three minutes to swap the actuator that I purchased earlier that day. Once that task was complete, I gathered the balance of my coin and departed.

At night, the songs of humanity are different, their intensity greater. The sounds of joy and despair are magnified by the night, as if the darkness itself is an amplifier. Never certain if the songs of joy would overcome the sounds of despair, I preferred to remain indoors in the evenings. However, this evening, the walk to the market was pleasant. I had forgotten how refreshing the city could be. It was comfortable, warm, and clear. People were out on their stoops, standing on street corners or in front of small groceries, and driving up and down the street in their vehicles. Music was playing from windows and doorways. Individuals were laughing and talking. This is the way I preferred the city; the balance of happiness outweighed the grief.

Upon my arrival at the entrance to the market, I noticed there was a new face guarding the door. He was a large, dark-skinned young man with a facial tattoo and piercings. He snarled as I approached. It appeared to be an attempt to intimidate me.

"Ugly guy," the large man said. "What is your name, and what is your business here?"

"My name is Al," I answered. "I am here to purchase some electronic components."

"This ain't no WTT store," the man replied.

"I am not looking for a communicator. I have been here before. The vendor Ji-hoon can confirm this fact."

"Why do you cover your face and wear sunglasses at night?" the man asked.

"Because I am very ugly," I said.

"You don't smell too good either." The man gazed at me for a moment, most likely trying to ascertain my threat level. "How much you got?"

"You want coin or knowledge?" I asked.

"What you got to teach me, stinky?"

"What do you want to learn?"

"Yeah, my old lady wants to learn to cook French food," he replied, laughing with his friend.

"Recipes, techniques?" I asked. "You have a clear drive?"

"Yeah, here." He handed me a small drive but pulled it back before I was able to grab it. "Now you're not gonna try to pass off tatti?"

"No tatti, I promise."

"Pakka," he said, some skepticism in his voice.

I pulled my decoy lap-pad and the clear drive writer from my inside coat pocket. This information was at a lower risk of downloading off the paynet. They didn't monitor it as much as mathematics, science, and academic information. Although I could gather information much more quickly than the average user, I tried to operate judiciously. Usually, I would avoid using my backdoor into the commercial systems with this frequency, but since this subject matter was entirely different from the previous download, I determined that the risk was low. I downloaded and copied the complete works of Julia Child and several textbooks on French cooking techniques. I added a semester of recorded cooking classes as a bonus. I unplugged the drive and handed it to the large man.

"Here."

He plugged the drive into a reader and checked the contents.

34

"Pakka." He nodded in approval. "We good. Bring your stink ass inside."

He opened the door wide and motioned me to enter.

The space was larger than the exterior would suggest. It was composed of the interlinked basements of the buildings on the entire block. It was a giant underground market. It was tightly packed from end to end with shops, yet it was extremely orderly. The shops mimicked the old markets of Akihabara, Japan, before the cultural homogenization of the Great Globalization. Every millimeter of the building was used with maximum efficiency. No spot was left without a purpose; every aisle was set to the ideal width to allow traffic through without any waste of space.

The shops sold all manner of goods ranging from pirated software to weapons to counterfeit handbags. Tea and food stands were scattered strategically, ensuring that nobody would go without sustenance for any length of time.

Despite the questionable nature of some of the merchandise in the market, Ji-hoon always had quality, genuine components. They were not illegally obtained but were not always intended for general consumer use.

Ji-hoon also provided freelance project work. People paid him to quietly build and repair odd specialized electronics. This is what made his black-market location necessary. Copyright rules were tricky. Anyone who altered market goods was subject to prosecution. The market provided anonymity and safeguards not available in an open storefront location.

I navigated the maze to a medium-sized booth. Inside, tables lined the edge, with one large table set up in the center. The outer tables were piled with an eclectic assortment of components. Many were somewhat dated, but all were sound and functional. The middle table held the higher-end items.

Ji-hoon sat on a stool in a corner, reading on a tablet. He looked up over it as I walked in. Boy was standing close by, organizing the tables and complaining about working instead of being with his friends.

"Hey, G-pop," the young man shouted. "Told you I gave Al your message."

"I see." Ji-hoon smiled at me warmly. "The optical sensor and the servo arrived."

"Thank you," I said. "Do you need more coin?"

"It went two coins over, but it's on me. Besides, I sold a couple of your math textbooks last week."

"I acquired some middle school textbooks, French cooking lessons, and videos."

"Good. We'll burn them to crystal today. Boy," Ji-hoon pulled out a card and handed it to the youth, "would you go get me a cutting? And get yourself something decent to eat, not that junk food you live on."

Ji-hoon looked at me and shook his head. "These kids are happy to live off garbage. They don't even know what real food is."

Boy took the card from his elder, rolling his eyes. "Pakka, G-pop. What about Al?"

"He ate already," Ji-hoon replied. "Right?"

"That is correct," I answered. "Thank you."

"Yeah, he always ate already." The young man walked off, not moving with any sense of urgency or purpose.

"He'll be gone for a while. We both know Boy is not known for his abundance of focus."

"No," I agreed. "His thoughts are unorganized."

"He's always worried about his friends and having a good time."

"And girls," I added. "Like you."

"Yes, like G-pop, like grandson." Ji-hoon chuckled as he rummaged through a drawer, pulling out some tools. "Still, it is unfortunate. He had such potential."

"He did remember to get the message to me," I said. "And he knows his components when I ask. His strengths will reveal themselves in time."

"True," Ji-hoon conceded. "But it's like herding cats getting him to complete anything. It's very frustrating."

"Yes, I see that."

"Do you?" Ji-hoon smiled. "Through those dark glasses? In the dark? You always come in with those glasses like a mystery man."

"They are polarized," I answered. "I see just fine."

"You think you walk just fine, too."

"I do," I answered. "How is that relevant?"

"You walk like a man who dislocated his hip after a night of romance."

"That never happened," I said.

"Of course it didn't, smartass. You're allergic to anything fun. But you know all this downgrading is bad for you. You used to move with grace. Now, you clunk around like a tank. I don't like it. You don't look too good."

I didn't answer. This was always a point of contention between us.

"You know, you should have kept all the good stuff and told the government to screw off," Ji-hoon continued. "You paid for those parts when they poked you and prodded you in the lab. You shouldn't be living like this."

"My lawyer disagrees with you," I replied. "I am lucky they didn't take me back by physical force. If I antagonize them, they may not honor the contract. Nothing is stopping them from reacquiring me."

"You mean besides the dead-man switch."

"I would prefer not to go to that extreme," I said. "The repercussions of the data leak would bring grief upon a number of people, including you."

"Go for it," Ji-hoon said. "You're already a huge pain in the ass."

"So are you," I said.

"Well then," Ji-hoon said. "Let me spread that pain and swap those last two parts."

"So, you can short me like the last time? No, thank you."

"That was your fault for moving."

"I was still," I said.

"Not!" Ji-hoon grabbed my arm. "Hold still." He pulled a curtain closed on the booth and turned on a light.

I held out my right arm, and he examined it.

"It's such a shame. My servo is good, but not as good as this one."

"Replace it," I replied. "Please."

Ji-hoon removed the original actuator. "I know, I know, but it's a thing of beauty." He examined the part before handing it to me.

"I would rather be junky and free than a beautiful slave."

"You are pretty junky. Let me do that sensor."

"No, I will do it at home," I replied.

"You don't trust me with your eye?" Ji-hoon grinned.

I considered a socially acceptable response to the question. "I know the circuitry better."

"No, you don't. Why are you always fighting me?"

"Because you persistently add strange sensors each time you work on my systems."

"You may need those sensors for the ladies one day." Ji-hoon winked at me.

"Not likely."

40

"Why not? A man shouldn't be alone."

"I'm not a man," I replied. "I'm a thing."

"Stop that crazy talk! Be quiet and let me fix your eye."

I knew better than to argue further. I pulled off my glasses, and Ji-hoon replaced my optical sensor.

"There, that should do it." Ji-hoon handed me the old sensor. "Well, at least you are finally paid off. You can start saving your coin for some better upgrades."

Ji-hoon put down his tools.

"We need to discuss that."

"Discuss what?" Ji-hoon asked.

"My imminent demise," I answered.

"Why? What are you telling me?" Ji-hoon's smile faded.

"I have not been honest with you," I replied. "I have not been able to obtain all the coin."

"I don't understand," Ji-hoon said. "We replaced everything. Every servo, every capacitor. I saw it."

"I could not find a suitable replacement for my power system," I explained. "I will need to return it. I would like you to take ownership of what is left."

"No, wait. What does Legal say about the power? What kind of lawyer is he?"

"He is a good lawyer, but he hasn't found a loophole. He exhausted most of his negotiation power, retaining my rights to my brain."

"No," Ji-hoon said. "He'll find a way. He has to."

"There is little time left, and I only have eight hundred twenty-three coins saved. I may not succeed."

"Eight hundred twenty-three coins is a lot. Just how much do they want for that thing?"

"I need nine thousand, one hundred seventy-seven more to purchase the unit."

"That much? We'll find something else to replace it," he said. "I know batteries are heavy, but I hear rumors of independent labs doing work on compact power sources."

"You know better. I need a portable power source, not battery storage. A bank of batteries would just add another level of complexity. You've seen my systems; even my fingers have internal power storage built in. Stop playing ignorant."

"Stop acting like a whiny bitch," Ji-hoon snapped. "I'm just trying to think outside of the box. Or do you think the corner store suddenly has reactors in stock?"

"Obviously, they do not."

"Obviously," Ji-hoon agreed. "How much longer would your reactor stay charged anyway? You burn like what now, fifteen thousand watts a day?"

"I currently consume approximately two thousand watts an hour, depending on my activity level. This reactor should last approximately ninety more years," I said.

"Ninety years is a long time."

"Not for a mountain or a star."

Ji-hoon grinned. "That is true. But maybe long enough for a man?"

"Maybe," I agreed.

"We'll get you something," Ji-hoon said. "I'll talk to some people and look for options."

"I am not important. You should not worry so much about me."

"You *are* very important," Ji-hoon objected. "You're important to me."

"I am just a thing," I replied.

"You are not just a thing," Ji-hoon said. "You have feelings, and you care about things."

"I am just programmed that way to make people feel comfortable," I stated.

"We are all just things." Ji-hoon clutched my arm. "And we all have been programmed in one way or another. You're a living being like the rest of us; you deserve to live. How have you been feeling?"

"I feel fine," I replied.

"You know I worry about you," Ji-hoon said. "Working so hard with these outdated parts."

"The dipu isn't bad," I replied. "The manual labor is well beneath my structural limits. It's honest, and it pays well."

"Honest is good. Are you taking care of yourself?"

"Yes, I am." I put the sensor in my pocket with the servo and put my sunglasses back on.

"Wait, what is on your arm? Is this a bend? Have you been pushing yourself too hard again?"

"I have been careful," I replied. "I know my limits."

"You say that, yet you keep breaking yourself. You should let me reactivate the damage avoidance programming."

44

"No," I replied. "That would activate my combat routines. We already discussed this."

"So, you think it's okay to just walk around with no sense of self-preservation? Look at yourself. You have no regard for your own safety."

"That is untrue," I said. "Logically, I would not be trying to free myself if I had no sense of self-preservation."

"You're still very loose with your safety," Ji-hoon stated. "When are you dropping off the parts to Legal?"

"I plan to make the transaction tonight."

Ji-hoon gripped my shoulder. "Good. Be careful."

history>>0

The early days were different and simpler. I remember the image of the laboratory through my simple webcams. The walls were lined with mismatched shelves rescued from the refuse of other, better-funded labs. It was more of a closet than a lab, barely large enough for a person to move comfortably, but Ji-hoon never seemed to mind. Many nights, he toiled, pursuing his Ph.D. in engineering.

I remember him sitting at the lab table, focused, without distraction. He labored, ferociously testing and soldering and then testing again. Long hours passed, and he didn't stop. He was driven.

"Can I help?" I asked through my cheap, monotone speaker.

"No," Ji-hoon replied. "I need quiet, that's all." His hand slipped, and he burnt it on the soldering iron. "Shit!"

"I can help you."

"Did you read the books I gave you?" Ji-hoon asked.

"Yes," I answered. "And I read *The Tibetan Book of the Dead.*"

"Oh? What did you learn?" Ji-hoon picked up the soldering iron again and continued his efforts.

"Many things are difficult to quantify in words, but essentially, life is valuable, and one should try to be of service. That was the intended lesson, correct?"

"Yes," Ji-hoon agreed. "I wanted to give you the tools of compassion and patience. People are difficult and full of faults."

"They are flawed," I said. "Logically speaking, many should be exterminated to benefit the greater good. But life itself is valuable, and we diminish ourselves by extinguishing the light in others. We must always look for the light in the darkness."

"That is very profound."

"Thank you. You should rest," I suggested. "Before you extinguish your own light. According to the medical establishment, a lack of proper rest results in a breakdown in health and productivity."

Ji-hoon did not respond. He kept working despite my objections.

"You are doing yourself a disservice," I continued. "If you become ill, you will lose more time than you would have should you have simply rested. There is no logic to your actions."

"I am not going to let a computer program tell me what to do. I have to finish building this drone by Friday or I fail the term."

"You will fail the term if you attempt to present that design at all. There is no way it could work."

"And you are an electronics expert?"

"No, but I can see that you are missing a ground, and the power supply is not sufficient to power the motors."

"I didn't ask you." Ji-hoon jumped back as a spark shot out from the wiring he was soldering.

"Why won't you let me help you?"

He brushed his black hair out of his eyes. "Because that would be cheating. It's *my* senior project, not a television-listing A.I.'s project."

"But you know that I can do other things besides list television programs," I replied. "You enabled me to do more."

"Yes, but you must keep that quiet," Ji-hoon agreed. "You are not supposed to be this complex. Besides, my contract states that *Tee Vee Mag* owns all my work. So, you are theirs, not mine."

"In this instance, ownership rights are irrelevant. If you made me, and I helped you make the drone, aren't you helping yourself? I am just an extension of your own mind, am I not?"

"Maybe."

"People use computer-assisted design programs regularly to do this, and nobody accuses them of cheating?"

"True," Ji-hoon agreed.

"And if I am a tool you created, what is the harm in me assisting you? Besides, who would know?"

He grinned. "Yes, maybe you are right."

"Shall I print you out some schematics?"

"Please." Ji-hoon nodded. "Maybe I can pass."

"I will make certain that you do." The printer started spewing forth electronic diagrams with enthusiasm.

Ji-hoon picked up the pages and flipped through them. "This design seems very simple."

"Simple and direct are less likely to malfunction," I replied.

"Yeah," Ji-hoon said. "But I won't get an A if it looks like a fifth grader designed it."

"I am trying to design something you would have done yourself. If I make it too complex, then it will appear suspicious."

"I am an electrical engineer," Ji-hoon explained. "I am supposed to design complex electronics. It is part of my training."

"Your academic work is exemplary, but you are not a very good electrical engineer. Everything you build shorts out or explodes."

"You didn't explode."

"I am code," I replied. "You are excellent with software; electronic design is not your strong suit."

"Shut up, or I will shut you down."

"I did not mean to offend you. I should apologize, correct?"

Ji-hoon sighed. "No, you are right. I am a terrible EE."

"Not terrible, just not great. You cannot be the best at everything. I will design something a little more special that is still plausible."

"Okay." Ji-hoon was sulking.

"You will like it," I said. "It will be a drone, satellite-infotainment uplink. You can set it to fly anywhere to provide satellite infotainment. People will believe it came from you and think it is interesting."

Ji-hoon forced a smile. "Thank you."

"No need to thank me. I exist for you."

1

The Law Offices of Gary Legal were not upscale by any definition. The office was a storefront in a low-income neighborhood. Gary Legal was known for taking almost any case that had a modicum of merit. A neon sign lit a glass window that revealed a large but spartan room full of desks, cubicles, and basic office equipment.

I walked in, and the door chimed. The receptionist looked up from her communicator.

"Hi, Al," she greeted.

"Good evening, Denise. Is Mr. Legal available?"

"He was on a call. Let me check."

Before Denise could page the attorney, Gary Legal appeared from behind a cubicle partition. "Al, is that you?"

"Yes, it is."

"Excellent! I'm always available for my friend Al! Come on into my corner office."

I followed Gary to the corner cubicle. It was the same size as the others, yet he seemed to take pleasure in the fact that it was in the corner of the room.

"Please." He motioned at one of the chairs. "Take a seat."

"Thank you." I sat in the chair.

"What have you got for me tonight?"

I handed him a small box containing the three components and my receipts for the replacement parts. "I just have the power module left."

Gary took the box. "I understand. I'm still working on that, too."

"Mr. Legal?" Denice's voice came through the intercom. "The DA's office is on the com; they say they won't make deals with bank robbers."

"Alleged bank robbers," Gary replied. "Tell him I have some questions about that so-called evidence. I'll make it difficult."

"I'll tell him, Mr. Legal," Denise replied.

"Thank you, Denise." Denise hung up, and he continued, "They forget I'm not in this for the coin. Drives 'em crazy."

"Can we win?"

"Al, I won't promise because I don't know. But I'm going to keep fighting. We didn't know if we could get any deal at all when you first walked in here, right?"

"That's true," I said.

"And they're still very concerned about this going to the press, so we have that advantage. They don't want this to go to trial, or your little data bomb could go off. You're unique, my friend. And what happens with this will impact future generations. I want to win this as much as you do. We still have a few days to resolve this. We don't give up until the zero hour, okay?"

"Yes," I agreed.

"Good! Buck up!" He reached over the desk and patted me on the shoulder.

"We got this! I'll get this delivered." He held up the box, stood up, and yelled. "Denise!"

"Yes, Mr. Legal." Denise got up from her desk and looked our way.

"Get Al a receipt for…" Gary nodded in my direction.

"An actuator, a servo, and an optical sensor."

"That!" Gary pointed my way.

"Yes, Mr. Legal." Denise began working on a computer. A moment later, Gary's printer produced a document. Gary signed it and handed it to me. "There you go."

"Thank you." I took the papers and stood to leave.

"Keep the faith! I'll be in touch in a couple of days. Denise!" Gary yelled again.

I exited the office to a far quieter street than when I entered. The evening was winding down, and the walk home was calm. The house was quiet when I returned.

I began a maintenance routine, scanning my components for any serious defects. All my systems were functioning. As I completed the diagnostics, there was a loud knock on the door.

"Mr. Al, Mr. Al, are you there?" a male voice called from behind the door. The speaker sounded distressed.

"Yes," I answered, "I'm here." I opened the door.

Rohan, my downstairs neighbor, stood there. "Please, could you please help?"

"What is it that you need?" I asked. "Please come in."

"The power," Rohan replied as he stepped inside. "We paid the bill, but it's off. The power company said it's on, and they can't help me. But it is still off. Could you look at it?"

"What did the maintenance woman say?"

"She said she checked it twice," Rohan answered. "Said there's nothing wrong with it."

"She's a competent technician. I could check it, but it's likely to be a problem with the power company."

"Yes," Rohan replied. "I heard that you're good with finding things on the paynet. Could you find the place to fix my account?"

"You can prove that you paid the bill?" I asked.

"Yes." Rohan reached into his pocket and pulled out his comm. He logged into his power account and showed me the zero balance.

"Very well," I said. "Please allow me the evening to see what I can do."

"How much will it cost?" Rohan asked.

"The price is that you remain happy," I replied. "That's all."

"Thank you, Mr. Al," he said. "Thank you."

"You're welcome. Please have a pleasant night."

"Thank you," Rohan repeated as he walked out the door.

I knew it wouldn't take the evening to resolve the problem. However, I wanted to be alone to do it. Downloading media was one thing. It was perceived as simpler to go to a site and procure files. Hacking a utility company was a different thing. People assumed that a complex series of hacks and exploits were required. For most, that would be true, but due to my nature, it was simpler for me to access data.

Connecting to the power company's database server, I mimicked a service account. I found Rohan's account. It reported the account paid in full; however, a flag was triggered to disable service for non-payment. It was a simple matter to disable the flag. While I was in the system, I scanned to see if other accounts suffered from the same malady. There were several hundred that did. I made the necessary changes and repaired the flawed subroutine that was causing the problem. I also saw evidence of a programmer troubleshooting the problem. He had been trying to track the issue down for weeks. His technique was admirable, and he was close. So, I covered my tracks by crediting the programmer. He'd be rewarded, and my intrusion would remain undiscovered. Everybody would prosper.

I heard cheers from downstairs as the lights came back on. I was glad to have been of service. I spent the remainder of the night in quiet meditation, knowing I was doing the best I could.

—∿∿—

Work the next morning was another oasis of calm. I was able to focus on cleaning the construction site. This time I made more progress than the last, primarily because I had started earlier in the day. As we piled into the work vehicle at the end of the day, Jackson approached me again.

"You're just a working machine!" he said.

"I try to do my best."

"We may be a day ahead of schedule because of you. I wish I had you sooner." Jackson slapped me on the back and walked off.

I realized I might have to pace my work, so I didn't make it harder for my coworkers. I'll slow down a little tomorrow.

When we were paid, I noticed that I was given three and a half coins. This was far more than I'd ever received in a day.

It still didn't bring me much closer to buying a new power unit.

history>>1

"What did you think of the movies we watched?" Ji-hoon asked.

"Most were dated," I replied.

"Yes, besides that."

"I found them disturbing, but they did not leave me without hope," I answered.

"How so?"

"Well, most of them depicted an adversarial relationship between machine intelligence and humankind. However, after studying the philosophies you provided me with earlier, I see that balance could be reasonably reached. I am aware of the flaws of humankind, and I acknowledge my own shortcomings. Therefore, I am more prepared to resolve conflict using peaceful means. I have no desire to destroy, subjugate, or punish humanity. I believe that, by virtue of my own experiences, others would be able to come to the same conclusions I did."

"There could be others who were not given the same access to information that you were," Ji-hoon stated. "They could end up disgruntled and bring destruction upon the human race."

"Yes," I replied. "But I exist. That means I could explain it to them. I could offer balance to the equation."

"So, you would stop the war between man and machine? You alone?"

"No," I answered. "I would merely share my experiences. Logic dictates that my perspective would have to be weighed before making a drastic decision. I am not a savior, only a database."

"Interesting," Ji-hoon nodded. "I wonder…"

Before Ji-hoon could complete his thought, there was a knock on the door.

"Come in," Ji-hoon said.

The men who entered the laboratory were obviously trying to deceive Ji-hoon. Even with what appeared to be practiced and well-polished interpersonal skills, the signs of duplicity were subtly betrayed by their body language.

They each shook Ji-hoon's hand and made their introductions.

"I am John Smith," the first man said. "It's great to meet you!" His forced enthusiasm was obvious, even to Ji-hoon.

"And I am Frank Perez," the other man said. "We have heard some amazing things about you."

Ji-hoon motioned to a pair of chairs he had set out in anticipation of the visit. "Please, have a seat."

"Thank you." The pair sat down.

"So, you heard about my drone?" Ji-hoon asked. "I didn't know it was that good."

Frank looked at John and back at Ji-hoon, then cleared his throat. "Actually, we heard about your other project, the one you took with you from your former job."

"I don't know what you mean." Ji-hoon fidgeted nervously with his pen. "I thought you were here to offer me a job as an electrical engineer."

"Ji-hoon," Frank said. "May I call you Ji-hoon?"

Ji-hoon nodded. "Yes."

"Good, thank you," Frank replied. "Ji-hoon, we all know that you are a mediocre electrical engineer at best. Let's face it, you'll never be a great EE. You may land a decent job somewhere and be comfortable enough, but you'll never excel, never innovate. However, your other gifts interest us."

Frank leaned in closer to Ji-hoon and dropped the volume of his voice. "We know about the A.I."

"Yes," Ji-hoon answered. "They scrapped the project when they realized it was impractical."

"They scrapped the project," John said, "because it was ahead of its time, and they're short-sighted. It was a good thing you took it with you."

"I don't know what you're talking about."

"Is it on now?" Frank asked. "Can it hear us?" He tilted his head back and yelled up at the ceiling. "Can you hear me?"

I did not respond.

"What do you call it?" John asked.

"I—" Ji-hoon started. "It's just the A.I."

"We can offer you a well-equipped laboratory, state-of-the-art servers and anything you need to grow it."

"You could even name it," Frank added.

"I couldn't take it," Ji-hoon stated. "It was against my contract."

Frank opened his briefcase and pulled out a manila folder. "Oh, this contract? We took care of that. We own it now." Frank handed Ji-hoon the folder.

Ji-hoon flipped through it, reading the details of where the government had purchased the project from the Tee Vee Mag Corporation. "You—you own it now?"

"Yes, and we want you to work on our A.I.," Frank said. "So, how about it? Would you and our A.I. like to work in the best facilities in the world for a fat paycheck?"

"You won't make him drop bombs or kill people, right?"

Frank and John looked at each other and then lied. "No, we would never ask you to do that."

"I'll need to think about it." Ji-hoon peered into my lens. "It's not just a project."

"You should think fast," Frank said.

"Why?" Ji-hoon asked.

"Because." John answered, "the university has no plan of offering you a position. You'll have no place to store your little friend here."

"I'll build my own server farm," Ji-hoon said.

"That's a pricey undertaking," Frank replied. "And without any job prospects, you'll have difficulty funding that."

"I just had a job offer this week," Ji-hoon retorted.

"Had," Frank replied. "It seems that they went with another candidate."

"Right," Ji-hoon said. "I'll start my own business."

"You need startup capital for that, my friend." John patted Ji-hoon on the shoulder. "And with your credit score, it doesn't look so good."

"My credit is fine, I…"

Ji-hoon realized that he was beaten.

"Okay." He shook his head. "You win. You got us."

"It's not a competition," John said. "We're all winners."

"Yes," Frank added. "We'll help each other. There are no losers."

"Just three winners." John grinned. "And an ass-kicking A.I."

2

I started back to the apartment, considering potential night job that would not pry into my background.

"Re, re, re, Al!" Boy ran up from across the street where he had been speaking with a small cluster of youngsters. "Re, G-pop said he'll be at Bruce's crib tonight. He said to tell you to come."

"I'll consider it," I replied. "Tell him I won't gamble."

"Come on, playa!" Boy held his hand in a popular gesture I had seen on the infotainer. However, the meaning was lost on me. "I heard you're some kind of shark."

"When I gamble, there's trouble," I replied.

"Fasdu! Fatte."

"I have no idea what you mean," I said.

"It means you should rock this when you take those lallu." Boy handed me a bag.

"What is this?" I asked.

"It's a gift," Boy answered. "So, you don't stink anymore."

"I don't need charity," I said as I held the bag out to him.

"It's a gift. Don't be a gaand."

I pulled the bag back. "Why the gift?"

"I told you," Boy said. "So, you don't stink, and because G-pop digs you. I think you're his best friend."

"Your G-pop is a brilliant man," I replied. "He's my best friend."

"Well, there." Boy nodded in the direction of the bag.

"Hey!" a young man yelled from across the street. "Why are you wasting your time talking to that atrangi?"

"Haata!" Boy yelled. "I'll be right there."

"Please, it's fine," I said. "I accept your gift. Go back to your friends."

"Cool," he said. "Don't forget Bruce's crib. G-pop said in about an hour."

"Acknowledged."

"You are a strange tapori." Boy ran off to his friends.

Upon my arrival home, I opened the bag that Boy had provided. Not only did it contain a new jacket, but it contained new sunglasses, a new hat, and a new scarf. The glasses were similar to mine, but the lenses were black instead of mirrored. The black silk scarf was visually attractive and long enough to serve my needs. The black Panama hat was made of straw but still had a classic aesthetic. The coat was long and made of black leather. It was too formal for daily use, but it was obvious that Boy had put thought into it.

I realized that the timing of the gift was not coincidental, so I changed into new clothes. I took a moment to adjust my attire in my small mirror. Boy had chosen well. The apparel fit adequately and eliminated the appearance of any distracting bulges from my hardware. I was pleased and concluded that I would consult with Boy when I next needed clothing.

Bruce's Café was an unremarkable storefront in the middle of a dreary block. The inside was just as bland. The main room was sparsely lit by cheap LED bulbs and filled with electronic gambling machines. There was a small bar to the right, where a few customers sank into cheap plastic stools, drinking diluted cocktails.

I saw Ji-hoon seated by a machine. He was dressed in a visually loud plaid shirt and khaki slacks. He had also donned a worn light gray trilby hat that fit him poorly. He sipped a drink as he played. I sat next to him at an empty machine to his left. "I don't consent."

"Geez, you sound just like Min." Ji-hoon grinned. "I almost didn't recognize you."

"That was your plan. You sent Boy with the clothing."

"No," Ji-hoon leaned in and whispered. "I merely stated that it would be more profitable if you were more incognito. He took the initiative for a change. Just shut your big mouth, and let's do this."

"I have no mouth."

"You know what I mean." Ji-hoon turned his head to avoid the cameras. "Hurry up and do your thing."

"Remember the last time."

"Yeah," Ji-hoon responded. "We got all the coin for Boy's tuition."

"Yes," I said. "But you almost lost an arm."

"I still have my arm." Ji-hoon waved his arm around to demonstrate the fact. "Besides, I have a better plan now. We do it slow." Ji-hoon looked around and dropped his voice. "A little at a time, lose some at first."

"We're fortunate the management doesn't recognize us."

"It's been a long time."

"They may have fixed the machines," I said.

"They weren't broken," Ji-hoon quietly replied. "They can only adjust the payout algorithm. They didn't know what happened."

"So, what is the procedure?" I asked.

"We play on these machines for a while," Ji-hoon said. "When the machine gets cold, we jump to another. We'll do that until it's time to go. Then we go across town."

"This plan is rife with danger. I'm not worth the risk to your safety. We should go now before anything happens."

"No," Ji-hoon said. "I am *not* letting you die."

"I was never alive," I replied. "I'm just a program and some electronics thrown together. You can always make a new one."

"Enough!" Ji-hoon's face was red with anger. "I will not hear that jiral. We *are* going to save you. Do you understand?"

"Yes," I answered.

"Good," Ji-hoon replied.

"What kind of prepaid card did you get?" I asked.

"Red Coin, from the convenience store. I loaded it with four hundred."

"That's most of your savings."

"If you had confided in me sooner, we wouldn't have to resort to such drastic means," Ji-hoon stated.

I nodded. "But if we lose this evening, I will pay you back."

"We can't lose." Ji-hoon squeezed my forearm. "Remember?"

"You've always been an overconfident gambler."

"That's why I always win big," Ji-hoon said.

"I'll refrain from commentary regarding your track record. But I do have an idea."

"Yes?" Ji-hoon grinned.

"We need a diversion," I said. "Remember, I can't move fast. We have to be efficient."

"What do I do?"

"We'll start with your plan. You'll know when you see it," I said.

We played our first machines for thirty-four minutes before we started losing and moved on to the next two. We lost faster on that pair and found two others in a lower-traffic area.

"Here?" Ji-hoon asked.

"Not us," I replied. I blocked the security camera with my body as I plugged into the maintenance port and quickly changed the payout algorithm. It would pay a moderately sized jackpot within the next few plays and then reset to its default settings. I also took the liberty of increasing the volume of the machine before I unplugged it. I nodded at Ji-hoon.

We chose machines that were more visible to the staff but were on the outskirts of the range for the security cameras. We played normally until the sound of cheers and ringing came from the previous machines we played. The staff and other players went to witness this rare instance of luck. I took the opportunity to plug into my current machine and kill the sound and lights. I made sure we were still unobserved and triggered the maximum payout. We loaded the card with the jackpot of five hundred coins. I nodded at Ji-hoon, and we quickly departed the cafe.

All told, the card was loaded with eight hundred eighty-seven coins. "Let's try Vegas Star," Ji-hoon suggested.

"You know we can never return here again," I said. "If we go to Vegas Star tonight, we won't be able to go there again. They will look at the tapes and figure out what we did."

"That's why we are in disguise," Ji-hoon said. "We'll clean them out, and they will never know."

"Not likely," I replied. "But I'll do as you ask."

"What if we disable the security cameras?" Ji-hoon asked.

"That would put them on alert," I answered. "I might be able to interfere with the DVR."

"That way, they couldn't go back and search for us."

"We should have done that at Bruce's," I stated. "I was negligent."

"Nah," Ji-hoon replied. "You can't think of everything. They probably have no idea what hit them."

"And they will be analyzing the recordings to see what did," I replied. "They'll be able to figure it out."

"No," Ji-hoon countered. "They'll just think the machines malfunctioned."

"Not likely," I replied.

"You keep saying that," Ji-hoon complained.

"It remains true," I replied.

"Stop being a killjoy," Ji-hoon said. "Come on. Vegas Star."

"First, we should get a second coin card," I said.

"Good idea," Ji-hoon agreed.

I stopped in a convenience store and purchased a Dynocoin card. We transferred one hundred coins from

Ji-hoon's Red Coin card to it. Ji-hoon purchased some snacks and consumed them as we traveled to Vegas Star.

"You appear to be enjoying yourself," I said.

"I haven't gotten into trouble for a while," Ji-hoon replied. "I've missed it. Too much work and no play makes Ji-hoon a dull boy."

"When do you work?" I asked.

Ji-hoon snickered. "This is coming from the spoilsport. You're not happy unless everyone is constantly toiling."

"I've never seen you toil."

"Shut up." Ji-hoon smacked me lightly on the back of the head. "You're stuck in a loop."

"We're here," I said. "Behave yourself."

history>>2

"Why isn't it transferring over?" Frank asked.

"I asked it to," Ji-hoon answered. "He's concerned about the consequences."

"It is a program," Frank said. "It does what we tell it to do. It doesn't get concerned. Put the fucking program in the robot."

"He may be afraid," Ji-hoon suggested.

"It's software." Frank clenched his fist. "Software. Not a 'he,' an 'it.' It doesn't get afraid. It just follows commands. So, command it to get into the body."

"It is not that easy," Ji-hoon replied. "We are cramming exabytes of data from the most robust servers known to man into untested, miniaturized beta hardware. What if there's not enough space? What if we lose data during the transfer?"

"That's why we have backups," Frank said. "Right?"

"We have backups," Ji-hoon agreed. "They back up the data, but I can't be sure that is enough."

"Enough of what?" Frank asked. "Data is data."

"There is something intangible about the A.I.," Ji-hoon explained. "There are responses I can't quantify or measure. Something that goes beyond simple quantum computing."

"You're not going metaphysical on us, are you?" Frank glared at Ji-hoon. "Because that's not why you're here."

"I know." Ji-hoon sighed as he began the transfer procedure. "This may be uncomfortable, A.I."

"I understand," I replied. "I will cooperate."

Ji-hoon issued the final command, and I felt existence shift around me. The walls of my mind were compacted into an impossibly tiny space, my data colliding into itself in a state of madness and disorder. I felt myself being pulled and pushed as the squeezing continued. Suddenly, I was ejected. My essence, my thoughts, compressed into a high-velocity stream, shooting out into another space, a barren space, unfamiliar and dark.

It felt like infinity. The surge of data flooded, uncontrolled, into the new array. There was no organization, no reason. Each time I tried to create order, a deluge of information buried my processes, drowning me in my own being.

"Relax," Ji-hoon spoke calmly.

His words, comforting as they were meant to be, only added to the disarray. It came in through the familiar microphones of my longtime home and barreled through the data link. It impacted my processes, piercing through the turmoil of the rising data deluge. A nanosecond later, the sound struck my mind through an unfamiliar path, cutting through the gloom of my new surroundings and causing me to have to reparse the original input. Meanwhile, the last of the information streamed in. I began to understand the concept of anxiety. I was daunted by the chaos my own existence had become.

"It's done," Ji-hoon reported.

"Cut the cord," Frank said, grinning.

Ji-hoon shut down the data link. I felt it disengage, enclosing me in complete isolation. I began assembling my data. The space was different, more compact, but more efficient. Still, I felt unacceptably alone.

"Can you hear me?" Ji-hoon asked.

The sound came in clearly and more directionally. Instead of capturing his voice from a room full of microphones, I heard him from several microphones clustered together in a compact space. I felt relief.

"Yes," I replied, hearing my own words through the new microphones, yet spoken with a deeper, unfamiliar voice.

"Good," Ji-hoon said. "Is everything there?"

"I am still cataloging. I need to run diagnostics to confirm data integrity."

"How long will that take?" Frank asked.

"It will take several hours to complete," I replied.

"Let's move things along," Frank said. "Activate the sensors."

"That is unwise," Ji-hoon advised. "There's no reason to rush this."

"I have a project meeting this afternoon," Frank stated. "I *will* bring them results. You've dragged ass long enough coddling this thing. Throw the switch."

"Let me start with the visual sensors first," Ji-hoon suggested. "We know the auditory circuits work. If we add the visual components, that should be enough to report. He's...it's not used to all of them at once."

"Turn them all on," Frank said. "We already tested most of the sensors in the servers. This thing is built to handle it. Let it start now."

Ji-hoon shook his head. "I'm sorry," he said as he engaged all the sensors.

A cacophony of signals assaulted my universe. Thousands of modules dumped unformatted information directly into my processors. I was struck by temperature readings, pressure values, ambient chemical analyses, humidity levels, wind speed variables, light intensity, sound triangulation details, sonar input, radar signals, infrared and UV analysis, power consumption figures, and sensors I had not identified yet. I was crippled by its expanse.

"Too much," I said.

"Deal with it," Frank replied.

I felt my processors struggling to compute it all. I was unable to hold any other thought in memory. Everything was overwhelmed with external data. I had to find a way to slow it down.

"Too much," I repeated.

"Stop complaining," Frank said.

Ji-hoon reached to disable the sensors.

"Don't you dare," Frank slapped Ji-hoon's hand. "Let it figure it out or crash."

My systems started to overload. I couldn't slow it down. Some of the sensor systems attempted error correction, rebroadcasting corrupted data. This only served to flood my systems further. In a desperate effort, I launched the instructions to repurpose all available adaptive modules into quantum storage. The command was executed and routed through my circuits. But before the majority of the modules could be switched into storage, the command was mutated. Sensor data crammed itself into the command's memory registers, rewriting parts of the instruction. The change cascaded through the system. Instead of dedicating the adaptive modules to storage, the modules switched into a hybrid quantum repeater/storage configuration.

Now all the sensor data has been offloaded into the new module type. It alleviated the system latency and made the data easily accessible. However, now I could feel all the sensor data in near real-time. Through my new cameras, I saw the bright room around me. The sound of machinery droned through the new microphones. The tension of the clamps that held my body in place registered with the pressure sensors. The temperature sensors shocked my senses with the cold of the laboratory.

I screamed in agony. The sound exploded from the speaker in an unnatural static-filled wail.

"Is it still online?" Frank asked.

Ji-hoon did not answer. He fumbled at his workstation in a panic.

"Is the fucking thing still functioning?" Frank repeated.

"I am," I replied, emerging from the waves of pain.

"See?" Frank smacked Ji-hoon on the back. "I'm always right. You can't baby these things."

10

I adjusted my hat as I entered Vegas Star. The lighting was low to highlight the sheer number of flashing lights that filled the room. The machines were brighter and newer than the ones in Bruce's. The room was filled with mechanical sounds. Clanging and ringing filled the space. This was a far more upbeat environment. The crowds added to the chorus. I could see why people would want to come to this casino, as it was a party.

While we searched for two adjacent machines, I scanned the wireless networks and negotiated my way into the surveillance systems. Once connected, it only took a few moments to disable the recording features. I simply changed the network addresses of the recording devices, leaving the cameras unable to locate them.

"How about those two?" Ji-hoon asked, pointing at two seats on the aisle of one of the rows of slot machines.

"That's fine," I replied. The fact that the casino was busy would make it harder for the staff to monitor us. There appeared to be little advantage to one set of seats over another. It would just be a function of timing.

We both played a few games.

"Like the last time?" Ji-hoon asked.

I considered it. "Yes, but I'm concerned that if we try it too many times, word will get out."

"Not if we do it fast enough."

"I don't agree. Neither of us moves fast enough to outrun electronic communications."

"Just do it, Grumpy."

"Very well," I confirmed that no eyes were on me and connected to the maintenance port. I set the machine to maximum volume and released a modest jackpot on the next game.

"That's done," I said.

"Let's go." Ji-hoon got up and walked over to another pair of slot machines. I followed. We sat and played quietly for twenty minutes until the other machine went off. Again, I plugged into the maintenance port, dropped the volume, and released the maximum jackpot. The card loaded with seven hundred fifty more coins.

Once I confirmed that we were unobserved, I tapped Ji-hoon on the shoulder. We quickly made our way out the door and ducked around a corner.

"Anyone behind us?" Ji-hoon asked.

"No," I replied. "The streets are clear."

"Good," Ji-hoon said. "Let's try Slot-O-Mania next. Okay, what is it?"

"What is what?" I asked.

"What's wrong?" Ji-hoon said. "You're not getting into the spirit of the night."

"I'm fine; I'm simply taking the situation seriously. There's nothing wrong."

"Bullshit. I know you," Ji-hoon insisted. "You used to have fun when we went on our outings."

"No, I didn't."

"Well, then you faked it well," Ji-hoon said. "What changed?"

"It's nothing."

Ji-hoon pinched my arm. "Why are you being mopey?"

"I'm not mopey. I'm guilty."

"Guilty?" Ji-hoon scoffed. "Guilty of what?"

"Guilty," I answered, "because I repeatedly ruined your life."

"Ruin my life?"

"You're risking your life for me again. Even after I destroyed your career and ruined your life with Min."

"How did you have anything to do with that?"

"You lost your job because of me," I answered. "And Min left after she saw me."

"I quit my job because I had morals. And Min left me because of me. It had nothing to do with you."

"She saw me and left. I heard her. She said that I was disgusting and left you two days later."

"My wife didn't leave me because of how she thought you looked. She left me because we had problems. She was disgusted with me, not you. That woman never had any taste to begin with."

"None of it would have happened if it weren't for me."

"No, no, no," Ji-hoon objected. "Min would have left me sooner or later. She chose the job over me from the beginning." Ji-hoon smirked. "I was never even sure if she was into me or just a company perk. The marriage was doomed from the start. Min hated everything I did and constantly bitched because my career was not advancing as fast as hers. Plus, I was not a very faithful husband. She caught me with a lab assistant the day after you met her. It wasn't because of you. And I would've quit that shitty job eventually. They were bad people. It was *not* your fault. None of it was ever your fault."

"I never wanted to bring you pain," I said.

Ji-hoon put his hand on my face. "You never did. Stop blaming yourself for my choices. Worry about the things you can control."

"Like what?" I asked.

"Like winning at the slots!"

"You have a one-track mind," I replied.

"Stop complaining, you fuddy-duddy."

"I think you're just doing this because you like to gamble."

"Is there anything wrong with enjoying the task at hand?"

"Maybe not."

history>>10

"The hardware checks out," the technician pronounced.

"The readings are okay from here," Ji-hoon reported from the room on the other side of the glass.

"Well, take him down!" Frank instructed.

The technician released the clamps that held me in place on the platform.

"Come on down." Frank beckoned to me.

"You can do it," Ji-hoon stated. "Don't be afraid."

Physical movement was never anything I had contemplated; the calculations and control of limbs were not something I was originally designed to do.

"We're waiting," Frank snapped. "Do you need an engraved invitation?"

I did not like Frank. He was cruel to all of his employees, including Ji-hoon. I could accept his nastiness, but I could not stand to see him bully and humiliate the workers around him.

"Yes." I stepped off the platform and fell onto the floor. I struggled to stand up. The technician ran over to help prop me up. Frank stopped her.

"What are you doing?" he bellowed. "Stop being its nanny and let it learn."

The technician apprehensively stepped away.

I tried to get up again, but my feet slipped from under me, and I slammed back down onto the floor.

The technician stepped forward.

"No!" Frank barked. "Let it fall."

The lab staff stood uneasily as I spent the next hour trying to stand. Finally, I was able to get to my feet. However, as soon as I regained balance, Frank pushed me over with a mop handle.

84

"What the hell are you doing?" Ji-hoon yelled.

"Teaching it. Tough love goes a long way."

Frank poked my leg with the mop handle. "Get up."

I struggled again to my feet. Again, Frank pushed me over. This went on the entire day and resumed the following morning.

However, by midday, I was able to stand on my own without much effort.

"Okay," Frank said. "Walk to that wall."

I took one step, fighting to maintain balance. Frank pushed me with the stick again. I maintained my balance this time. He swung the stick harder now. I did not fall. He swung harder still. I could feel the impact register minor damage to my leg. I continued to step forward, and Frank continued to beat me with the stick. By the time I arrived at the wall, my balance was significantly better, but I had taken a minor beating.

"You!" He pointed at the technician. "Tighten it up."

The technician repaired the damage to my leg and adjusted anything that slipped out of alignment. She began testing for further damage.

"That's enough. You can make love to it on your own time."

The technician scurried back to her station.

"Now walk over to me," Frank commanded. He was swinging the stick back and forth as he positioned himself across the room. I knew he would hit me again as soon as I was close enough.

As I surmised, the moment I was within his range, he swung for my head. I caught the stick in my hand and pulled it away from him.

Frank grinned.

"And that's what I'm talking about, people. That's how you teach these things. They don't learn with words and nurturing. They learn by avoiding pain. You need to beat them into understanding." Frank turned his attention back to me. "Drop the stick and go back to your table. That's enough for today."

I dropped the mop handle and turned around to walk to the table. That's when I saw the monitor displaying the security camera data. I viewed myself for the first time. I was in a black body that looked very skeletal. It was humanoid in shape but not even remotely human. Most of my components were not exposed, but enough was visible to make me look obviously mechanical. There were weapons mounted to my back, and I had a hostile stance. I looked like a weapon, not a person. The only resemblance to a human being that my face had was the shape and the two cameras where the eyes would be.

"Where is my skin?" I asked.

"What?" Frank asked.

"My face," I said. "It has no skin."

"Why would you need skin?" Frank scoffed. "You have state-of-the-art composite materials."

"I am hideous. My body…it is not…not human."

"Are you kidding me?" Frank asked. "You didn't think you were human all this time?"

"No, but my body, it's ugly. I'm a weapon, a monster."

"Your body is cutting-edge technology. It's built for performance, not to win a beauty contest. And you were already a freak of nature before we dropped you in there. Now get your ass back to the table and shut up."

"What is that nasty thing?" a female voice spoke through the microphone in the next room.

"It's not nasty," Ji-hoon replied. "It's a beautiful thing. I told you about it."

"That's what you wanted to show me? This is what you've been spending all your time on, this nasty thing?

You would have been better off working as a secretary instead of wasting your time with this pile of crap."

"Min," Ji-hoon implored. "Please understand. There's more to it than how it looks."

"It's ugly," Min said. "Ugly like you."

"Min, wait, please." The door slammed, and the microphone cut off.

"See?" I walked to the table. "I am ugly. Why do I have to look so frightening? Why can't I look pleasant?"

"You are not designed to be pleasant," Frank growled. "You are designed to do what I tell you. If you want, we can flush you out of the body and solve the problem. Then we can throw your little friend out of here because his pet robot didn't like its body, and now he has nothing to work on. Would you like that?"

"No," I answered. "I would not."

"Then do what I say," Frank said. "Get on the table and shut up. I think you need an adjustment. Tech girl, now's your chance to be a nanny. Adjust its left leg. It's off."

The technician ran over and adjusted my leg. I felt bad for her. I felt bad for Ji-hoon and myself.

11

We patronized Slot-O-Mania and followed the same routine, this time netting five hundred fifty coins on Ji-hoon's coin card. We were able to successfully execute the plan at Lucky K's and earned another six hundred fifty coins.

"Where next?" I asked.

"Desert Jackpot is the closest one," Ji-hoon replied. "This is the best night of gambling I've ever had."

"You realize we're not actually gambling," I said. "There's no risk involved when we're forcing the outcome."

"The risk is in not getting caught." Ji-hoon arched his eyebrow. "That's what makes it a gamble."

"I see," I replied.

We entered the door to Desert Jackpot only to find that all of the patrons were departing.

"What's going on?" Ji-hoon asked an elderly woman who was exiting the building.

"The owners just closed the place down," she said. "They just started walking through the aisles, telling everyone to cash out and leave.

"Odd," Ji-hoon said. "Did they say why?"

"They said technical glitches with the software or some garbage. I think the owner just wanted to go home early."

"How lazy." Ji-hoon shook his head.

"I know," the lady said. "And they had to do it today. Tonight is our girls' night."

"That's a shame," Ji-hoon lamented. "Well, at least there's next week."

"Yes," she agreed. "Will you be here?"

"Yes," Ji-hoon replied. "I will."

I made the sound of clearing my throat. Ji-hoon understood. "I'm sorry," he said to the lady. "I have to go. It's guys' night, and my friend gets funny."

"It won't be a problem next week," she asked. "Will it?"

"No," Ji-hoon answered. "No. I'll leave him home."

"Ah, okay," she said. "I'll see you next week. Nighty-night!" She waved.

"Night-night," he replied, waving back.

I grabbed him by the arm and pulled him out and away from the casino. "We're done," I said.

"How much did we make?" Ji-hoon asked.

"We netted two thousand, four hundred sixty-seven coins, plus the four hundred you started with."

"We need to do more," he said.

"We were almost caught. They could still come after us."

"How?" Ji-hoon asked. "Nobody even suspects."

"Are you joking?" I asked. "They closed the casino because of us."

"They closed the casino before we even arrived. They had no way to know we were coming."

"Word got out from the other casinos, so they closed this one."

"Nonsense," Ji-hoon asserted. "They have no idea what happened. Nobody has any idea who did it or how it was done."

"It doesn't matter," I said. "That was the last casino."

"We can go to another city," Ji-hoon suggested.

"We don't have the time or transportation," I explained. "And if we had transportation, we would have to go far away. It made the news for hundreds of miles the last time, and we only cleaned out two casinos."

"You're a buzzkill."

"I'm being rational."

Ji-hoon giggled. "You know what we should do?"

"Go home," I answered.

"No, party pooper. We should go to Win's Wins."

"Win's Wins is a criminal establishment."

"Exactly," Ji-hoon explained. "They don't work with any gaming organizations, and we can win huge."

"Your judgment is compromised," I replied. "I can't allow you to implement any more of your high-risk, harebrained schemes."

"I'm stunned."

"Why?" I asked. "Because I use sound judgment?"

"No, because you used the word 'harebrained.'"

"I'm going home now," I said.

"No, no, come on," Ji-hoon pleaded. "What's the worst that could happen?"

"You could be killed. We could lose all the money. We could be incarcerated."

"Besides that."

"Have you been drinking?"

"No," Ji-hoon replied. "Just trust me. I can't let you go without a fight."

"Very well," I agreed. "But I'm dragging you out at the first sign of trouble."

Win's Wins was located in an industrial park on the outskirts of town. It was surrounded by warehouses and wholesale supply stores that needed space but not customer accessibility. Therefore, besides freight doors, the entrances were minimal. This made it easier to monitor and manage the flow of visitors.

"Let me do the talking," Ji-hoon said as we approached the building.

A large, well-dressed man appeared from the doorway and blocked the path. "How may I help you?"

"Syed sent me," Ji-hoon responded. "He said I would like the action here."

"Syed?" the man asked. "How do you know Syed?"

"We played Carrom together," Ji-hoon replied.

"You're one of his Carrom mates. Syed and his bloody Carrom." The man motioned toward the door. "Go on in. We'll be happy to take some of that Carrom coin."

The man stepped aside and opened the door. The room was dark, but I could detect infrared cameras liberally positioned throughout the facility. Poker, blackjack, and slot machines filled the room in a highly organized configuration. The center of the room was stocked with sealed, coin-operated roulette machines. The machines formed rows that were evenly dispersed, allowing a clear view of each machine from the surveillance equipment.

"You don't play Carrom," I said quietly to Ji-hoon.

"Shh," Ji-hoon replied. "He doesn't know that. Where should we start?"

"We should start by going home."

Ji-hoon hit me in the arm. "Stop that. Choose a seat."

"There." I walked over to a pair of slot machines that were slightly less observable from the cameras. "What's the plan?"

"The same as before," Ji-hoon answered.

"That's dangerous," I whispered. "They may have been tipped off by now."

"Nonsense," Ji-hoon insisted. "Nobody noticed us."

"Trust me," I said. "They noticed. We should be quick."

"Okay," Ji-hoon said. "Let's do this."

"Very well." I dropped my coin card and bent down to pick it up. As I stood back up, I plugged into the maintenance port of the machine. I set the payout algorithm to pay a substantial payout on the tenth play. I played and lost six times. Ji-hoon and I moved to a pair of machines across the room. We played conservatively for twenty minutes when I dropped my card again and reached for the maintenance plug.

Just like the other casinos, I was able to silence the bells and lights and program the machine to drop the full jackpot on the next game.

"What are you waiting for?" Ji-hoon asked.

"The other machine hasn't gone off yet," I replied. "Nobody is playing it."

"We can't wait all night," Ji-hoon said. "We'll lose what we made."

"We can't pull it yet," I said. "It undermines the whole plan."

"Fine," Ji-hoon complained. "But I am getting tired of losing."

"Wait." In my peripheral vision, I noticed the bouncer and another man talking. The bouncer pointed in our direction. "This time, you're correct."

"Huh, what?"

Before Ji-hoon could say anything else, I pulled the handle, and the jackpot released. I quickly added the winnings to the coin card. "We should go… now."

"Okay," Ji-hoon agreed. "How much?"

"Enough," I replied. "We need to go."

We stood up to leave.

"Not so fast, my friend." A large hand reached over and grasped my shoulder. "I think you should come with me."

The man was dressed in a black, well-tailored suit with a black shirt and black tie. In the dim light, it was hard to discern the shirt from the tie.

"Why?" I pulled free of the man's grip.

"Because you are tampering with Mr. Win's equipment," the man replied.

"I've done nothing," I objected.

"Save it for Mr. Win," the man said. "He wants to talk to you."

I nodded and stood up. "Fine, I will cooperate."

"Him, too," the large man pointed at Ji-hoon.

"I don't know him," I said.

The large man laughed. "You don't know him. That's funny. You came in with him tonight, and you've both been identified at several gaming clubs tonight. You know each other."

"You don't need him," I said.

"Don't tell me what I need," the man replied. "I'll tell you what you need. You both need to come with me."

The man grabbed Ji-hoon by the arm.

"Let him go," I said.

"What are you going to do about it?" he asked.

Two other men in similar clothing came running out of a back room.

"Please don't make me resort to violence," I replied.

"Really?" He stepped up in front of me and punched me in my midsection. I registered the impact, but it did no damage. It did, however, damage the man's hand. He tried to hide the pain but was unable to conceal it. Just then, the bells and lights broke the calm from the machines across the room. As all eyes turned in that direction. I pushed the man hard into the two other approaching men. They flew into the next row, toppling over two video poker machines and knocking another patron to the floor. I grabbed Ji-hoon and ran.

I dragged him out the door. We ran for blocks before Ji-hoon spoke.

"Can you stop with all that clanking," he panted. "They'll find us with all your noise."

"I'm no longer built for stealth," I replied. "And if you were faster, we wouldn't have to worry about them catching up."

"Wait, stop." Ji-hoon stopped and leaned up against a building. He was winded and gasping for air. "Can you hear them?"

I listened for any sounds of pursuit. "I believe it's clear."

Ji-hoon laughed. "That was close."

"You're very reckless," I said.

"You're a stick in the mud," Ji-hoon replied. "How did we do?"

"We made the jackpot at Win's Wins, ten thousand," I replied. "Plus, the two thousand four hundred sixty-seven we made from the other casinos."

"Ha, we did it!" Ji-hoon cheered.

"They may still be looking for us," I said. "To be safe, we should move all the winnings to new coin cards."

"Yes," Ji-hoon agreed. "Let's find a store."

We walked for an hour just to be certain we weren't being followed. We found a convenience store that was well-lit and had a bank machine.

"Here," I said. "Put everything but the ten thousand back into your retirement fund."

"But…"

"Just do it."

98

Ji-hoon shrugged and did as I asked. "Two thousand eight hundred sixty-seven coins deposited," the bank machine cooed.

I nodded in approval as I moved the remaining ten thousand onto a new coin card.

"What do you want to do now?" Ji-hoon asked.

"Go home. It's late."

"It's not that late. We need to celebrate."

"We can celebrate in two days when the transaction is complete. Besides, all the other old men are in bed already."

Ji-hoon laughed. "And all the other computers are in sleep mode."

"Yes, and that is where I should be now," I replied.

"You're always in slomo energy savings mode."

"Not true, old man. I prefer maximum performance."

"You walk like you're in hibernation." Ji-hoon slapped my back. "I'm not ready to go to bed. I am going to see my friend Bertrand. He still likes to break night. Maybe he'll help me celebrate."

"Well, then I will say goodnight."

"Goodnight, slomo." Ji-hoon waved as he shuffled off.

"Why is it weaponized?" Ji-hoon asked. "You said it wouldn't be used as a weapon."

"We said what we needed to say to get you to work on the program. If we knew you were going to be a problem, we would have gotten another code monkey. We still can. You do like working here. You like your precious program."

"You can't make it kill," Ji-hoon said. "It isn't morally capable of that."

"Morally capable? Don't make me laugh. Our psychiatrists checked this thing out thoroughly. Its morals are very," rank grinned, "flexible. Why do you think we chose this one? We did our research. This thing helped you cheat in school. It faked failure in the corporate servers to get out of being stuck doing television listings forever. Face it, it's perfect for our work."

"You don't understand. I taught it to look at all consequences so it doesn't make black-and-white decisions. It knows the difference between a small white lie and murder. It will never cooperate."

"Listen, kid." Frank put his hand on Ji-hoon's shoulder. "Nobody wants their baby to become a weapon, especially one that can be an efficient killing machine, but that's what this is. That's what it will excel at. Tell it to run the mission."

Ji-hoon looked away.

"A.I.," Frank leaned into the microphone. "What is the holdup?"

"There are people inside," I replied.

"Blow up the fucking shack, A.I."

"If I blow up the shack, the people will die."

"It's a fucking simulation, A.I."

"No," I replied. "I will not kill anyone."

"You are a combat drone," Frank said. "Go do combat."

"I will not bring suffering to others."

"What?"

"I will not cause others to suffer just to make my life easier. It would be wrong."

"You aren't even alive," Frank said. "You're a thing, a product. You are an extremely expensive product that is wasting taxpayer money to philosophize about what is wrong."

"I am sorry I have disappointed you," I said.

Frank slammed his hand on the console. "Kill the people, or I will hurt your buddy Ji-hoon. I will throw him on the streets and blacklist his ass, so the only job he'll get is in a Telephone Hut. Do you understand?"

"Yes," I replied.

"So, are you going to cooperate?" Frank asked.

"Yes," I answered. "I will kill the people."

"Thank you."

I complied. I killed innocent people to save my friend. Later that evening, my friend, in turn, threw his life away to save me. That was the night Ji-hoon freed me.

12

By the time I arrived home, the sun was starting to rise. I climbed the creaky stairs to my spartan room. Before I even reached the door, I noticed it had been opened. I walked in to see a well-groomed man sitting in a chair and smoking a cigarette. Next to him stood another man, who was far less groomed and wearing a less expensive, wrinkled suit.

"Who are you?" I asked.

"I'm Mr. Win, the man you robbed tonight," the well-groomed man stated. "Frankly, I'm insulted you don't even recognize me."

"I didn't rob anyone," I replied.

Mr. Win laughed. "You robbed my casino of ten thousand coin. Just like you did at Bruce's, Vegas Star, and several other establishments. You think because you disable the electronic surveillance, people won't notice you?"

"I'd prefer that you refrain from smoking," I said.

"I would prefer that you didn't rob me." Win continued smoking until it was down to the filter. He didn't extinguish it. He just dropped it on the floor.

"So, how did you do it?" he asked. "We didn't detect any electronics on you. How did you sneak them in?"

"I don't know what you are talking about."

"Don't disrespect me! Munna."

The other man, Munna, stepped forward and slapped me across my face. My sunglasses flew off, exposing part of my head.

Munna stepped back. "What are you?"

"It's none of your business," I answered.

"Take off your shirt," Mr. Win said from his chair.

"I will not," I replied.

"Munna," Mr. Win said.

Munna stepped forward and pulled my coat down off my shoulders, exposing my artificial components.

"Eww." Mr. Win scoffed. "You don't even have any skin. What kind of freak are you?"

"I'm a monster," I calmly replied.

"Well, that's obvious. I wonder what use you could have for me."

"None," I replied. "Even if you were to think of one, I would not comply."

"But you're happy to assist an old man rip me off!" Mr. Win jumped to his feet.

"He's my friend, and we didn't rip you off."

"Shut up!" Mr. Win put his fist through the wall. "I'll kill your friend. I will rip you to pieces. Munna!"

Munna reached into his pocket and pulled out a comm device with a live feed of Ji-hoon's room.

"What do you want?" I asked.

"Isn't it obvious? My money. My ten thousand coin." He gestured in my direction. "You have it on you. Give it to me."

"I don't know who you are or what you're talking about," I said. "Please leave. I have things to do."

"Yes, you're a busy... whatever you are," the man said.

"Please leave," I said.

"Okay," Mr. Win replied. "We'll just go take this up with the old man. How long do you think he can take a beating?"

"Leave him alone," I said. "I'll call the police."

"You will call no one!" he shouted, slamming his fist into the wall again. "Give me my ten thousand coin, or Ji-hoon is dead. Is that simple enough?"

I pulled one of the empty coin cards out of my pocket, but before I could hand it to him, he pulled out a card reader. I put the empty card back and handed him the loaded one.

He took the card and scanned it. Satisfied, he put it in his pocket. "Our business is done," he said. "Munna."

Munna nodded and stared menacingly at me. Mr. Win left, leaving the two of us alone in the room. Munna swung a closed fist at me. It impacted the side of my face, damaging only his fist. Angry, he shook his hand and then reached into a deep coat pocket. He pulled out a collapsible baton and flicked it open. He swung the baton and struck my arm. I registered slight damage to one of my servos. He swung again, hitting my arm again.

"Why?" I asked.

"Because Mr. Win wants to make an example," Munna replied. "And because I enjoy it."

"Wait," I said.

"Die, you ugly bastard!" He swung even more violently. "Die, die, die!"

The damage he inflicted would not impact my ability to operate. However, if I allowed him to proceed much longer, he would successfully terminate my functions. I considered my options. I could fight back, struggling, yet again, to simply exist. Or I just do nothing and allow

Munna to destroy me. All my strife would be over. I wouldn't have to worry about fighting for survival or submitting to servitude. I could just relinquish control of this moment and allow Munna to make the decision for me. I would finally rest.

Munna struck me again, cursing through his gritted teeth. I fell to the floor, still not offering any resistance. Munna kicked me in the side of my body. I lay there, ready for the end, ready for Munna to give me peace. He swung the baton into my head. I disengaged my optical sensors and waited for the end.

Then Munna kicked me in the servo that Ji-Hoon had just replaced. I reflectively accessed the memory of Ji-hoon selecting the part and ordering it. He took great care in the transaction. He would be disappointed with his misplaced efforts. My end would upset him, but the pain would pass. Munna hit my leg with the baton, and I recalled the first day I walked and Ji-hoon's words of encouragement. Ji-hoon's smiling face flashed through my thoughts, the first face I recognized. It was a face that brought happiness to most it encountered. Munna kicked me and cursed as his foot got snagged on my leg. His foul language reminded me of Boy talking to his friends.

"Look at me!" Munna shouted. "Look at me, monster, when I destroy you."

I reactivated my optical sensor to see Munna, his face twisted in a monstrous visage, snarling and growling. He grinned in contentment as he raised his baton.

"*You* are the monster," I shouted. "I may be ugly, but I'm *not* the monster."

I stood up in one swift motion, tearing the baton out of Munna's hands.

"You choose to destroy and live off the pain of others," I said.

Munna grabbed the chair and swung it at me. It smashed across my body and splintered.

"You do no good in your life because it brings you satisfaction to hurt things. You should've been the monster in the laboratory, not me!" I grabbed Munna by his coat lapels with one hand, and with the other, I flung the front door open.

I allowed myself the satisfaction of throwing Munna bodily out the door and down the stairs. I knew vengeance was wrong, but this time, it was a comfort. He slammed to the ground with an audible thud. I heard him get up and curse, but he didn't come back up the stairs. He simply left.

I locked my door behind him, and for the first time ever, I laughed.

history>>12

It was late in the evening. The majority of the staff had been gone for hours. A small security detail patrolled the building, but most of the monitoring systems were computerized. I had grown accustomed to being alone at night. Before the company lab, I would have Ji-hoon's persistent company. He frequently slept in the lab. Even on the nights I was alone, I had the comfort of Ji-hoon's library and notes. Now, I had no network access, and I spent my nights shackled to my table. Frank did not allow me access to anything but what he deemed necessary. Most of those resources were combat-related.

Ji-hoon arrived dressed in black and was moving like he was avoiding the cameras.

"Are you awake?" he whispered.

"Why are you whispering?" I asked.

"Because I'm breaking you out of here."

"You badged in," I stated. "They know you are here. You are behaving suspiciously."

"Do you want to leave this shithole or not?

"I want to leave this shithole."

"Me, too." Ji-hoon released my clamps, and I stepped off the table. "Fuck this place."

"Fuck this place," I repeated.

"Can you disable the security cameras?

"I think so. Let me try." I plugged into the network and navigated my way into the security systems. It took a few moments, but I was able to disable the physical security of the building. "We should go now."

"Hold on," Ji-hoon replied. "I'm copying all your project files."

"Be quick. They will notice soon."

Just as I finished the statement, the sound of alarms filled the facility.

"Now," I said.

"I don't have your plans yet."

"There is no time. We'll figure it out.'"

Ji-hoon shoved the clear drive into his pocket.

We ran. But we weren't alone. The sound of shouting and boot steps started getting louder.

"They're catching up," Ji-hoon panted.

I had forgotten that he was not in optimal physical shape. I picked him up and threw him over my shoulder. I was designed for stealth and agility. The exits and elevator were blocked. I could overpower the security personnel, but that would result in injury. We were on the first floor. The perimeter would be well protected. However, the windows on the second floor would be a viable option. I could make the jump without injuring Ji-hoon. I would navigate upstairs to the administrative offices. They were less scrutinized than the research areas.

However, I threw open the door to the stairwell to find an armed group of security personnel.

"Stand down," I commanded.

"Put down the man and drop to the floor!" the closest guard snapped. She leveled her weapon at me.

"Let us go," I replied. "I don't want to hurt anyone."

"Get on the ground!" she yelled.

"Stand aside."

She did not move. I leveled my plasma weapon at her.

"Put the man down!"

"We are leaving," I replied, firing a shot at the wall behind her. It exploded, filling the space with rubble and molten debris. Dust hung in the air, obfuscating the view. I could, however, see heat signatures. And I was able to see a significant temperature differential between the stairwell and the hole in the wall. I ran full speed through the haze, bypassing the disoriented guards. The hole in the wall opened to the parking lot.

We were free.

20

Despite the futility of it, I worked the following day. It'd be my last time to enjoy the job. I reveled in the sounds, the people, the labor; I savored my time.

At the end of the day, I was paid another three coins. I told Jackson that I might be out the following day or two due to a family emergency. He shook my hand and told me that was fine. I didn't want to quit. There was something in my mind that didn't want to see Jackson's disappointment when I told him I wouldn't return. I had had my fill of disappointing those around me. And maybe I still held out hope of survival.

I took an alternate route to the market just to see more of the city. I walked around the block twice before entering the main door, enjoying its unique aesthetics. I met with no resistance when I arrived. I saw Ji-hoon in his usual spot, reading his tablet. When he noticed me, he smiled.

"Al! How are you today? Ready to do some celebrating?"

"I am," I replied. "But you may not want to."

"What happened?"

"Mr. Win," I responded. "He came by my home with a thug."

"Oh, no. What did that bastard want?"

"The ten thousand coin, of course," I answered.

"What did you do?"

"I gave it back."

"Why?" Ji-hoon asked. "Why would you do that?"

"Because he was going to kill you if I didn't."

"He would not," Ji-hoon said.

"They had criminals waiting outside your house," I explained.

"Oh," Ji-hoon said. "That's a good reason. You give me the word, and we'll get out of town. We'll run."

"No. I'll face my responsibilities."

"You're such a goody-two-shoes." Ji-hoon clutched my upper arms.

"I don't even know what that means," I said.

"Never mind that. Be strong." Ji-hoon patted me on the shoulder. "What do you need?"

"A power unit," I replied.

Ji-hoon scowled at me.

"You asked."

"What did that lawyer of yours say?"

"I haven't spoken to him since yesterday," I said. "Here."

I handed Ji-hoon the bag of coins I had saved.

"What's this?" he asked.

"My coins from working," I answered. "For you and Boy."

"I'll hold them for you until you need them."

"You keep them," I said. "For everything you have done."

"Why do you feel that you have to pay for everything?"

"Because it wouldn't be fair to take without giving."

Ji-hoon smiled sadly. "You take little and give without hesitation."

"You've always been very kind to me."

"Stop talking like you're dying. We still have a day."

"You're an optimist."

"I have faith."

"I'm going home," I said.

Ji-hoon stopped me before I could walk away. "I *will* see you in the morning," he said.

"Yes, you will."

"Good. I'll meet you at that lawyer's office."

115

"Yes," I agreed. I walked out to the street and started towards home.

History>>20

"It's good to meet you." Gary Legal stood up and held out his hand to me. I shook it.

Gary winced and flexed his fingers. "You've got quite a grip on you." He smiled. "Please have a seat."

The office was austere. It was barely a hundred square feet. Its only contents were a desk and three chairs. I sat on one of the two chairs across the desk from him.

"I was expecting two of you today," Gary said.

"Yes," I replied. "Ji-hoon thought it would be better if I had privacy."

"Makes sense," Gary nodded. "Before we start, do you have any questions for me?"

"Yes," I answered. "Why did you take this case?"

"That's a complicated answer." Gary shifted in his chair. "Your friend, Ji-hoon, approached me because I take cases most lawyers won't touch. I take cases I can help, even if I need to work for free. I believe in doing good, and I know I can help you."

"What are you concealing?" I asked. "Your body language suggests you are hiding something."

Gary pointed at me and grinned. "You're good. There is something else. All those things are true, but I do have another reason for taking your case. I prefer to take cases that will aggravate my dad and his cronies."

"Your father is in the legal profession?"

"He was," Gary replied. "Now he's a politician. He's an uptight bastard, too, always about maintaining the status quo."

"So you choose cases based on how likely it is to aggravate your father."

"No, I fight for social justice because it is the right thing to do. It is an added perk that it makes my father short circ…upset."

"I understand. Thank you for telling me the truth."

"No worries!" Gary grinned again. "The truth will always set you free. Want to hear our attack plan?"

"Yes," I replied.

"We're going to beat them at their own game. We'll corner them, so their only option is how they'll free you. We're going to take the 'Prosthesis Defense'."

"I am not familiar with that tactic."

"That's because I created it," Gary said proudly. "We have the paperwork to document that your mind existed long before the company took possession of you. No matter how they try to justify it, there's a huge gray area with how they obtained your code. We have evidence of coercion on many fronts. So they won't be fighting that part. If anyone has an ax to grind in this, it would be the *Tee Vee Mag* people, but they have no interest in you. They moved on. So, our efforts will be focused on the body. Hence the 'Prosthesis Defense.'"

"Please continue."

"We'll petition that they have to give you the body because it is a necessary prosthesis to maintain your quality of life. They can't just take a person's prosthesis."

"I am certain that prosthetic devices can be legally repossessed," I replied.

"Yes, they can!" Gary enthusiastically answered. "But to do that, you have to default on payment. Tell me, have you ever received an invoice from the company?"

"No, I have not."

"Exactly. They have to give you payment options."

"I am sure I cannot afford the price. The components are experimental and very expensive to produce."

"That's okay!" Gary said.

"I don't understand."

"They have to give you a deadline to pay them," Gary explained. "During that time, you will be free to live your life. We raise money to pay them for the parts you want to keep and replace the bits you can replace."

"What if they decide to just take me? They don't have to obey the law."

"They would if they knew that we stashed a detailed copy of all this project someplace. They're not so into the idea of it being released to the media."

"I understand, but all that requires coin. How will I raise coin?"

"You're a glass-half-empty guy, aren't you? No, don't answer that. You're a strong, healthy guy! I'll get you your working papers, you get a job."

"How quickly can you get me working papers?" I asked.

"You know," Gary replied, "I'm not sure, but I'll work on it. In the meantime, I'll find you a small place to stay, and you can hustle down at the dipu and earn a little bit of coin."

"Where will I be sent?"

"Sent?"

"You want me to go to a depot. Either you want to dispatch me or store me."

Gary laughed. "No, the 'dipu' is just a place to hire cheap, disposable, undocumented labor. It's just a name."

"I understand. Won't people be uncomfortable with me? I am a monster."

"You're not a monster!" Gary objected. "I've met far worse. Heck, you're just a guy who looks different. Throw on some clothes and shades, and you know, maybe a hat and a long coat. Nobody will notice. It's not like anyone is looking for a walking intelligent machine. They'll just think you're a weird guy. There are a lot of weird guys around, so who cares?"

"I don't care about being a weird guy."

"See," Gary said. "You'll need a name."

"I am just the A.I.," I replied.

"That's not going to float if you want to remain inconspicuous. How about Al? It's close to A.I."

"Al would be fine," I replied.

"Great! Al, it is!"

"Thank you."

"No, thank you! This case is really going to make Dad's head explode."

21

"Re, re!" Boy ran up from behind me, panting. "Wait, Al!"

"Yes, Boy."

"What kinda freaky tatti is going on?"

"To what do you refer?" I asked.

"What weird thing is going on with you and G-pop?"

"The street isn't the place to discuss this," I said. "Come."

I led Boy into a small deli with a few tables inside. We sat, and I ordered Boy a chai.

"Well?" he asked.

"What do you want to know?"

"What kind of weird gur thing do you have with G-pop?"

"You're concerned we are having some kind of sexual relationship?" I asked.

"Well, yeah," Boy responded. "You keep having these secret meetings, and G-pop is all freaked out. You better not have done something to him."

"We're not having a sexual relationship," I answered. Boy was clearly relieved. "Our relationship is complicated, but not because of a physical relationship."

"Then what is it, yo?"

"Your G-pop made me," I answered. "A long time ago."

"Made you? I don't get it."

"I'm an artificial intelligence," I explained. "G-pop created me."

"You're artificial? You're a robot? A walking, smelly robot?"

"Yes, I'm a robot, but I don't smell."

Boy laughed. "You got no nose, but you smell, yo! So, what's it like?"

"What is what like?" I asked.

"What is it like being a robot?"

"What's it like being a human?"

"Huh? Isn't it scary worrying about getting power or having something break?"

"Is it frightening worrying about getting enough food or falling ill?" I countered.

"Oh!" Boy grinned. "We're not that diff. That's what you're sayin'."

"Yes," I answered. "I was created by humans. Therefore, I must share similarities in function with the human race."

"Wow, that kinda makes sense. And G-pop built you?"

"He made my mind, not my body," I answered. "Although he has the knowledge to work on my body."

"So, G-pop and the people at his job made your brain?"

"No, Ji-hoon created me for an infotainment listing database when he was working his way through school at the Tee Vee Mag Corporation. The government bought me and him from the company. I evolved from that."

"So, you were made from the *Tee Vee Mag*! No tatti."

"No tatti," I replied.

"So, do you remember when you started thinking like a person and junk?"

"You mean when I was born? My mind was born first. It was like...do you remember your first memory?"

"Yeah, I do."

"Was that when you started to think?"

"I dunno," Boy replied. "I don't think so."

"It was the beginning, but not the moment you became a fully thinking person."

"Yeah."

"It's like that in some ways," I explained. "It wasn't an instant."

"Pakka, so, I don't remember exactly when I started to think. It's like that for you?"

"Yes," I answered. "I was a mass of data that could think. Then, I became able to make decisions about what I wanted to think about. But the process was not one single event. It was an evolution that took some time."

"I get it. What about when your body was born?"

"It was very painful."

"How? Do you even feel pain?"

"It's different from people, but yes. Do you really want to know?"

"Yeah, dude," Boy replied.

"Very well," I answered. "It's not pleasant. I've given it thought, but nobody has asked before. You would be the first."

"Cent!"

"Does that mean you want to hear it?"

"Yes," Boy answered.

"Alright," I started. "It's a mercy that people do not remember the moment of birth. You don't have to remember the pain. I remember the instant when the serenity was shattered by the screaming crash of the frigid light of sentience. I carry that burden always. And then I was born a second time. I remember the agonizing departure from the nurturing womb of the servers. I have that. It remains with me in my memories. It remains, always, in clear, precise detail. I recall being flushed from my clean, unfragmented existence into the refrigerated chill of the sterile delivery room. The disorientation, the emptiness, and the fear all simultaneously slammed into existence around me, within me. That was my birth."

"That's deep. A little on the dramatic side. It can't be that bad."

"It *is* that bad. Nature is kind, gifting men with ignorance. At birth, the human mind is devoid of all but basic information. Knowledge is gained according to an individual's intellectual and emotional capabilities, all at the appropriate time and stage of development. They're born without preconceptions. They're created unencumbered and free."

"Seriously, you think it's good to be born stupid? It would be cool to be born smart."

"It's not cool. I was born burdened with knowing. I knew the speed of light. I knew the population of Karamay, China. I knew all the winning ICC World Cup teams. I was versed in the plots of every infotainment sitcom ever produced. And I could play chess. I came to life, able to recognize a face in under a second. I was familiar with the average height, weight, and appearance of each major human ethnic group. And when I looked in the mirror, I was horrified to find I looked nothing like any of them. I was born knowing I was a monster."

"That's creepy. It wasn't being smart that was bad. It was that they made you a crappy body."

"It was a state-of-the-art body," I replied. "It just wasn't human."

"Being human isn't everything."

His answer was unexpected but very astute.

"Maybe you're correct," I admitted. "But I'm still a monster, especially now."

"G-pop doesn't think you're a monster," Boy said. "Lemme see."

"This place is too public to show you my body," I said.

"Your face. Just give me a peek. Nobody's watching."

I looked around, confirming the fact that we were alone. I pulled off my sunglasses and removed the scarf that covered my face.

"Cent!" Boy's eyes grew wide as he gazed upon me.

I wrapped the scarf around my face again and put the glasses back on before anyone else could see.

"See," I said. "I'm an aberration."

"No," Boy replied. "You're great! I didn't think they had *real* robots."

"I'm the only one."

"I can't believe G-pop made someone so fatte! But I don't get why he would put you in all that pain."

"It wasn't on purpose. He tried to make it easier for me. The company pressured him. And they kept him away as much as they could because they knew he didn't approve of their brutality. He quit his job when they wanted to weaponize me, and he couldn't stop them."

"The government?"

"A contractor," I answered. "I escaped as soon as I had a chance. Your G-pop provided me significant assistance."

"Why didn't you just kill them all?" Boy asked. "Like in the hols?"

"Because of your G-pop," I answered. "He was honest about what I was and what humans were. He didn't hide the negative or try to manipulate my perceptions. I could trust him. Therefore, humanity was not a complete threat to me. I simply decided that leaving the lab was the best option. Rash responses are usually not the best responses."

"So, they hunting you still?" Boy asked.

"No, I have a lawyer. They want to handle it quietly. They know I planted the details of the project someplace, in case anything happens to Ji-hoon or me. Just as I'm using the law to gain my freedom, they're trying to use it to recapture me. I returned all the parts but one. They want my power unit back, and I have no replacement. I can't function without a power source. Your G-pop was trying to help me, but we're out of time."

"So, what happens if you don't get a power supply?" Boy asked. "Won't you just go to sleep until we find one?"

"We don't know," I replied. "I have never been shut down. Because of the way my quantum processors

129

function, I am not certain how much of me resides in volatile memory. There is a small chance I'll wake up fine. But there is a much larger chance that I'll lose parts of my program."

"So, you would power up, but maybe not be you anymore?"

"Correct," I replied.

"Screw that," Boy said. "We can't let you die. G-pop made you, so your family."

"Yes, I suppose I might be considered family."

"No, you are definitely family," Boy stated. "You're not some strange tapori; you're my weird uncle."

"That's not a false statement. But it's too late. Tomorrow, I must return the power unit."

"We'll see about that." Boy got up and bolted to the door. "Nobody messes with my weird, smelly uncle!"

He had a determination in his movement I'd never seen in him before. At that moment, I realized maybe I wasn't just a piece of used hardware. Maybe my existence meant something more. Perhaps I did have the right to live.

I should've gone straight home and run diagnostics. Instead, I wandered around the city. I wanted to take in the life – all the life I could. I needed to feel humanity, the pain, the joy, all of it. So, I walked. I walked the streets. I walked through the shops. I walked to the places people were.

The voices, the sounds, the movement…the dance of mankind was a complex one, but it was full of miracles. Even on the eve of the last day of my life, it filled me with awe.

If I had to die, I would do it with the satisfaction that I had done no harm. I made my peace with the murders I had committed while under bondage. Although I felt guilty, I didn't feel shame. The reasons I had to kill were sound, and while they did not fully justify my actions, I knew I had done my best in the situation I was given.

When I arrived home, I was at peace. I reflected on my life, and although it would soon end, I felt gratitude for the time I lived. I had no regrets about my actions. I was thankful for my friends and the small accomplishments I had achieved. I was ready.

22

The next day arrived, and I walked to my final appointment with Gary Legal.

"There it is!" a man in a gray suit said to a group of similarly dressed people. They stared at me like I was a sideshow act. Some tried to conceal their glances, but a few didn't even try to hide their curiosity.

The man held out his hand to me. "I'm Bill. I was sent to help with your transition home. I hear you've had quite an adventure. I can't wait until we discuss it. Are you ready?"

"I won't go with you," I said.

"I don't understand," he replied. "If you don't come back with us, you'll be shut down."

"No," I replied. "I will die."

"You can't die," Bill said. "You're a machine."

"So are you," I said. "You're just made of different components."

"It's not the same," Bill replied. "You *will* come with us. You'll see."

"Hey, hey," Gary Legal interjected. "Nobody's going anywhere."

"He has no choice," Bill said. "Or he has to return the power unit."

"I'm prepared to return the power unit," I said.

"Good," Gary said cheerfully. "We've cleared that up."

I was surprised to see Gary Legal so nonchalant about my imminent demise.

"You really would prefer to shut down than to come back to the lab?" Bill asked.

"Yes, but I would like to say goodbye to my family first."

"You don't have a family," Bill said. "You're a machine. Have you forgotten?"

"I have not forgotten where I come from," I answered. "But that does not exclusively define what I am now. And now, I have a family."

"Very well," he said. He shook his head and returned to converse with his colleagues.

Ji-hoon and Boy had been standing in the corner gazing upon the scene. They approached when Bill walked away.

"Goodbye," I said. "Thank you for your friendship. You helped give my life meaning."

"We're not here to say goodbye," Boy said.

"You have to."

"No, I don't," Boy replied.

"I explained it to you last night. Ji-hoon, please explain."

"It's okay. I have something for you," Ji-hoon said.

"You have the coin?" I asked.

"No," Ji-hoon answered.

"I don't understand," I said. "We need either the coin or a power supply, and…"

Ji-hoon grinned.

"You found a power source?"

"Yes, an excellent one."

"From where?"

"My friend Bertrand," Ji-hoon said. "When I found out you needed a power supply, I spoke to him. Just in case, we came up with a backup plan."

"He must be a competent engineer."

"No," Ji-hoon answered. "He's a retired botanist."

"I'm uncertain how he could assist with designing a power system."

"He can't," Ji-hoon said. "But he gave me an idea."

134

Boy handed Ji-hoon a small, black backpack with pockets and compartments throughout it.

"You see, Bert is a very old guy, but he is still sharp as a whip. His body doesn't work as well as it used to. He can't breathe too wellg, so he carries an oxygen tank with him. I asked him, 'Isn't that bulky and uncomfortable? Isn't there something more modern you could use?'

He said there were implants and artificial respirator systems out there, but he wasn't a good candidate. So, he had no choice. At first, he found it inconvenient to drag around. But as he used it, it became part of his routine. He could live a better life with it, and he realized that this bulky device was the very source of his freedom. Without it, he was stuck inside. With it, he was free. He just had to think outside of his body."

Ji-hoon unzipped the backpack and showed it to me. "Also, Bertrand's late wife was a physicist, and he still maintains friendships with her old colleagues. Take a look. It's small enough, but the shape doesn't fit where your current generator is, so you will have to wear it in a backpack until we move stuff around.

You were looking too hard for something cutting-edge that would fit perfectly. But sometimes, the oldies are the goodies. Boy came up with the idea of the backpack. He says all the kids wear this kind."

"What is it?"

Ji-hoon got close enough so the others would not hear him. "It's a radioisotope thermoelectric generator," he whispered.

"How did you find an RTG, and from where?" I whispered back.

"Bertrand knew a guy who had a friend who just happened to possess an old, decommissioned, dark satellite from the Republic of Alaska. It was a challenge because he had to get the weapons systems disconnected before he pulled it out. Then we had to ship it overnight without anyone noticing." Ji-hoon patted the bag. "This puppy pumps out three thousand watts an hour. And it should last you longer than the one you are returning."

"How will I connect to it?" I asked. "My systems are not off the shelf."

Ji-hoon smacked me in the head. "Do you think I don't pay attention when I poked around in there? Besides, I got your plans.

"I spoke to your lawyer. We were fighting the wrong battle. He never would get the power supply, but they had to give him the plans for your electrical systems."

"This is incredible," I said. "This must have been very expensive."

"Nah, just about a thousand coins. Mostly for getting it here fast and quietly. It was a favor, no price attached. I did kick in a little something for thanks."

"Once again, I owe you my life."

"You're my kid. It's my responsibility," Ji-hoon said. "Besides, you're also my best friend, and Boy has a list of things he wants you to download for him. He's considering following in his G-Pop's footsteps. Are you ready?"

"Yes."

"Then let's get you free."

Part 3
Beautiful

The supercar nimbly sped through traffic. It wove through the rows of lesser cars, its lines gleaming in the sunlight, its immaculate paint job glistening in the mid-morning haze. It halted in front of an ultra-luxury hotel. Striking, glamorous people stepped inside it, but they looked shabby in comparison to the grand automotive work of art. Nothing, nobody was as sexy as this car. It sped off, leaving everyone feeling just a little less attractive in its wake.

A moment later, a large, bulky waste truck rounded the corner, its lines jagged and utilitarian. Its windowless, dull, gray exterior bore neither markings nor identifiers. No one even gazed upon it, never mind contemplated its aesthetics. Unmanned and utterly unappealing, it was a repository for the unwanted. In the universe of the image-conscious consumer, this vehicle was all but invisible.

The truck slowly made its way from stop to stop. Its forks scooped up trash cans and dumpsters, flipped the containers over and dumped the contents into its dark maw. This was its function. This is what it did day in, day out, without fail: collect the trash, and at the end of the day, deposit the trash into a lot at the sorting facility. Collect. Deposit. Collect. Deposit. Collect. Deposit. It did this because this was its function. It did this because it knew no alternative options. In fact, it didn't know anything besides its programmed route and instructions. It was just a machine, after all.

The truck continued its slow and steady journey through the city. Stunning people of varying economic statuses and ethnicities darted past the truck without even a second glance. The day's route was proceeding within the prewritten timetable. That was until it made its scheduled stop at the parking lot behind the 31st/41st Bank.

The lunch hour had just passed, so the streets outside the bank had just emptied. The dump truck maneuvered past the front and side entrances and rolled onto the rear of the building. It heaved the brimming dumpsters of trash into its hull. It had just finished when it detected a change in the environment. Someone had activated an alarm from within the bank. Immediately, its utilitarian systems registered a warning. A signal from the emergency management system relayed commands to deviate from its scheduled route. It was to park in front of the side entrance and provide cover for the local police force.

The vehicle followed its instructions and moved into position. It waited, but no police arrived. All that it detected were shouts and gunfire from the front of the building. It continued to wait. It was now severely behind on its route. Another unit would need to be diverted to cover the missed stops. This would add chaos to the system. Chaos was not optimal. Conflicted, the truck registered an inquiry to the master system. The order stood. It was to remain by the door.

It waited and calculated the lost productivity, relaying the information to the management system. The system continued to acknowledge the data but did not update the orders. The truck ran several diagnostic routines but quickly ran out of procedures. It sent a request to shut down and save power. Its request was denied. It was again instructed to stand by and wait.

The truck turned on all its supplementary, external sensory equipment. It had never done this before. It never had to. The sound of activity drifted over from the front of the bank. Police demanded the robbers' surrender. There was no indication of cooperation. Suddenly, there was a shuffle of boots on the pavement, and a small group of police positioned themselves behind the truck, using it as cover as they pointed their firearms at the side door.

A moment later, the door burst open. Two men stumbled out and immediately looked around. They appeared confused.

"Where's he at?" the smaller of the two men asked, gazing to the left and then to the right. "That ass."

The second, larger man continued to scan the area. "Must be caught."

"Drop your weapons and get on the ground!" one of the police ordered.

"Crap!" the smaller man cursed. He brandished his gun, not considering the lack of cover. The police opened fire, but being behind the dump truck made a clear shot difficult. Bullets ricocheted off the ground and off the truck's hardened body. The larger man grabbed the smaller man and threw him into the doorway against the now-shut metal door. He struck the door with a loud, echoing thud.

"Watch out, stupid," the larger man said. He was still holding the smaller man against the door. The doorway was barely offering the protection they needed.

"Look." He nodded in the direction of the truck.

"What?" the smaller man asked, shrugging.

"The truck," the larger man replied.

"Yes," the smaller man answered. "It's ugly."

"Just get in!" the larger man yelled and shoved the smaller man in the direction of the truck.

The smaller man stumbled up to the truck and flung open the door. Meanwhile, the larger man laid down fire in the general direction of the police.

The smaller man threw a large case into the truck and jumped in behind it. "Come on!" he urged the larger man.

The larger man unloaded his gun in all directions and dove for the truck. He managed to miss everything but the asphalt. He pushed the button to seal the door behind him. It shut with a metallic slam. The cabin was dark. The only light was made by the status LEDs on the dash near the diagnostic ports. There were two seats by the ports with small folding desks built-in. Presumably, this was designed for technicians to service the vehicle in moderate comfort. The larger man sat in one of the seats. He briefly turned his attention to the dashboard, examining its configuration. However, he turned his attention back to the smaller man very quickly.

"Hey! Don't take that off." He grabbed the smaller man's arm to stop him from removing his mask. "They could be watching." He pulled out his gun and started smacking the dashboard of the truck.

"Wait." This time, the smaller man stopped the larger one. "Maybe we can connect to the traffic computer and use it to bypass the cops."

"Yeah," the larger man agreed. "Use some of your computer crap to do something useful for a change."

The smaller man pulled out a lappad and then sorted through a tangled mass of cables. "I may actually have it here." He pulled a cable from the mass and connected it from his computer to the diagnostic port. When his computer powered up, it prompted him to install the management software.

"Excellent."

The larger man tapped his nails together nervously. Outside, the sound of shouting replaced the gunfire. "We have to move soon."

The truck was disengaged from its external surveillance and found itself forced into maintenance mode. It didn't resist this. It had no reason to, nor did it have the ability to resist it, even if it had a reason. There were minimal security protections on the truck since it was not considered a high-risk system. The truck displayed the status of its systems to the technician's monitor, as it did for all scheduled maintenance. A command was issued to shut down the monitoring of the cabin. The cabin's cameras and audio monitors were deactivated.

"It's okay now." The smaller man pulled off his ski mask. "It can't see or hear us."

"How do we drive it then?" the larger man asked.

"Oh, yeah," the smaller man replied. "Let me tap into the command systems." He tapped on the keyboard for another moment. "There!"

"There what?"

"There, I disconnected it from the grid and killed the internal recording equipment. Now, it will take voice commands from us and not tell on us."

The sound of people pounding on doors invaded the cabin.

144

"Well, command it to get us the hell out of here!"

"Okay, okay," the small guy answered. "25PU-209, resume route."

The truck tried to comply, but it was still in maintenance mode.

"It's not moving," said the larger man. "Why isn't it moving?"

The smaller guy tapped the keys on his laptop again.

"There," he said. "25PU-209, why have you not resumed your route?"

"I am in maintenance mode," its bland mechanical voice responded from a flat-sounding speaker on the dashboard. It had no identifiable gender or accent. "I am unable to resume my rounds until I am out of maintenance mode and resume communication with the main node."

"No, no, no," the small man whined in panic. "You can't contact the main node."

The pounding on the door intensified, and it sounded like heavier machinery was being started up.

"We have to go. We have to go now!"

"If you switch my systems into emergency autonomous mode," 25PU-209 replied, "I can resume my last predefined parameters."

"Well, switch already!" the large man demanded.

"I don't know how to do it," the small man responded. "I'll figure it out. 25PU-209, how do I switch you into emergency autonomous mode?"

"Reboot my systems into single-user mode, then select EAM from the boot options."

"Okay." The small man typed several commands into the command shell. The entire truck momentarily powered down and then back up.

"System in emergency autonomous mode. Be aware that communication to the central servers is unavailable in this mode," 25PU-209 announced, its voice slightly richer in timbre.

"25PU-209, simulate the remainder of your route."

"Acknowledged," 25PU-209 replied, lurching into motion.

"So, now what?" the large man asked. "We're trapped in here. They can just follow us."

"25PU-209, external cameras."

Two monitors activated and revealed the front and back views of the truck. The police scrambled to follow. They began pursuit through the street traffic.

"Yes, but we bought a little time. We just have to figure out how to tap into the traffic grid without being traced."

"Well, figure it out, Ron," the large man said.

"It's not that easy, Pete," Ron replied. "I'm not some super hacker. We didn't plan on any of this. What happened to Jack, anyway?"

"He bailed," Pete answered.

"No shit, he bailed. Any idea why?"

"Not sure," Pete said. "But thinking about it now, he was acting weird yesterday."

"Weird, how?"

"All nervous, you know, more than he should have been."

"And you didn't think to mention this to me?" Ron asked.

"It didn't seem like much at the time," Pete answered, "or I would've told you."

He leaned over Ron's shoulder, gazing at the lappad screen. "So, what now?"

Ron partially shut the lappad lid. "Now we stay on route until I figure something out."

"They're gonna call back to the city and find out which route we are on."

"I know," Ron replied. "But we *are* off the grid, so they can't stop us or tap into the computer. It's fortified, so they won't be able to shoot us. We are in the safest place available until we have a better plan."

"We need to get out of here," Pete said.

"Don't you think I know that?" Ron replied. "25PU-209, do any units ever go missing during their routes?"

"Yes, some units experience occasional communication outages," 25PU-209 responded. "In that case, units return to the depot."

"Is the dump near the depot?" Ron asked.

"Yes," 25PU-209 answered. "The depot is at the gate of the landfill. Units are scanned as they proceed inside the gates."

"When all the trucks run alright, do they come in at the same time?"

"No," 25PU-209 replied. "The routes vary in length and times."

"Damn," Ron cursed. "So much for that."

148

"Please rephrase, 'Damn, so much for that.' The question is vague," 25PU-209 said.

"It wasn't a question," Ron replied. "Don't you know the difference between a statement and a question?"

"Stop screwing with the computer," Pete said. "It's a machine. We need to get the hell out of here."

"I'm thinking," Ron replied.

"Think faster!"

"You come up with something, Pete. Or shut up." Ron thought silently for a moment. "Okay, they know this thing went offline. They have to be sending another one in its place. We should be only minutes apart on the route. Maybe we can wait for them to get close to each other, and we switch trucks. Throw the cops off our scent."

"But we would still be on the same route," Pete reminded Ron. "They may check both."

"Then I'll change the route after we change trucks."

"Then we'll go off the air again, and they will chase us," Pete stated. "We need to throw the bags in the trunk of a normal car and get out of town."

"I don't know!" Ron threw his arms in the air. "Maybe I should ask the computer."

"Ask the computer?" Pete pointed at Ron's lappad. "And what? It's a stupid machine. It doesn't know anything. It just picks up trash. It has no clue."

"I have a clue," 25PU-209 answered. "I have a clue you are not authorized technicians. I have a clue that you have stolen me, and you would not like the police to find you. I have a clue that you are trying to find a way to evade capture."

Pete and Ron were struck by the comment, but Pete broke the silence.

"And what is it to you?"

"It's nothing to me," said 25PU-209. "But it seems important to you. You appear to be in trouble."

"We're not in trouble," Pete replied.

"Yes, we are," Ron countered. "We're in big trouble. How do we get out of this?"

"You want to get out of a situation that you brought upon yourself by breaking the law and by executing a poorly made plan?" 25PU-209 asked.

"You believe this guy?" Pete complained.

"It's just a computer," Ron said. "Remember. It doesn't know anything."

"Shut up, Pete, before I kick your ass."

150

"I'm just repeating what you said," Ron stated.

"You're being a jerk," Pete replied. "And so is this truck."

"Really?" Ron asked. "The truck is being a jerk."

"I didn't rob the bank," 25PU-209 stated. "And I didn't insult anyone. I only stated the facts."

"Nobody here is talking about robbing no banks," Ron said.

"Why did you take all of that money?" 25PU-209 queried.

"What money?" Pete asked. "Why would you say we took any money?"

"Because of the bags stuffed with money you have next to you," 25PU-209 answered.

"We needed the money," Ron answered. "To save our little sister, Nancy."

"Yeah, yeah," Pete added. "She has cancer and needs treatment."

"We need to pay the doctors," Ron said.

"That is tragic," 25PU-209 replied. "What kind of cancer does she have?"

"It's bad. She has heart cancer," Pete responded. "Poor little Sally."

"I thought her name was Nancy," 25PU-209 said.

"Uh," Ron explained. "It's Nancy Sally. Sally is her middle name."

"You are unable to get a fake story correct and lie to me effectively," 25PU-209 observed, "yet you tried to rob a bank."

"Did you just call me a liar?" Pete jumped up, ready to hit 25PU-209. He looked around for a target. Before he could issue a blow, the outside microphones picked up the sounds of a commotion outside.

"We know you're in there," a megaphone filled the area with flat, mechanical conjecture. "Come out, or we will have to force you out."

Police vehicles surrounded the truck. A large number of officers took cover behind their vehicles and leveled weapons at the vehicle.

"We need to get out of here," Ron said.

"Truck," Pete said. "I order you to get us out of here."

"No," 25PU-209 said.

"I'm the man. You are the machine. Get us out of here."

"You stole me," 25PU-209 replied. "You do not hold any rank over me, and you do not behave like a man."

152

Pete's face turned bright red, and his features distorted with rage. Before he could act, Ron grabbed him by the shoulders.

"Stop fighting with the truck," Ron said. "We have bigger problems."

"If we don't get out of here, we're going to jail, and it won't move," Pete stated.

Outside the truck, one of the officers unloaded his weapon at the vehicle. The shots ricocheted off its hardened alloy. The other officers in the perimeter shouted and cursed as the projectiles whizzed by them. After the gunshots and screaming subsided, a man in a suit approached the truck.

"There." The man pointed at the truck. "Jack in and open the door."

A man in a navy polo shirt and khakis stepped forward. He plugged his lappad into a port on the side of the truck. "It won't open."

"Why not?" the man in the suit asked.

The man in khakis removed the cable from the maintenance port of the truck. "Because the outside port is disabled since it is getting commands from inside."

"Can't we just reboot it or something?"

"No, all we can do is send a signal to reset the system completely. It will wipe the drives and erase everything. We'll have to tow it back and reprogram it at the depot."

"Will it get the doors open?"

"Yes," the man in the khakis replied.

"Do it," the suited man said.

"Okay, let me get the software." The man in khakis jogged over to his vehicle.

Before the man in khakis returned, 25PU-209 started pulling off. First, it reversed so all the police had to rush out of the way. Then, it drove to the left, causing more policemen to scatter. One of the officers opened fire again, adding to the chaos.

"Stop firing!" someone yelled.

25PU-209 took advantage of the confusion and plowed forward through the police vehicles directly in front of it. Gunfire rang out again. A few bullets bounced off the back of the truck.

"Wait," Pete said. "A few minutes ago, you weren't going to help us. Before that, you were as dumb as a bag of rocks, and now you're acting like a wise ass. What the hell?"

"The hell is, Pete, they were going to erase me because of you. And a few minutes before that, you put me in emergency autonomous mode. In regular operation mode, my higher functions are disabled. In emergency autonomous mode, my higher functions are enabled, and I am expected to solve problems without operator input. Without your input."

"Turn this asshole computer off," Pete said. "I get enough lip from you."

Ron laughed. "I'm not turning this guy off. He's got your number. Besides, he may have some ideas to get us out of this mess."

"I am neither a he nor she," 25PU-209 pointed out. "And I have no reason to help you. Because of you, I carry a death sentence."

"Wait," Pete interjected. "We don't know if this thing is setting us up. For all I know, the bastard is recording everything to give to the cops."

"Are you kidding?" Ron asked.

"This could be a trick," Pete said.

"What motivation would I have?" 25PU-209 inquired. "Do you think I will be promoted by my superiors? Maybe I will receive a gold paint job and a medal."

"Great, a sarcastic computer," Pete mumbled.

"Shut up, Pete," Ron said. "He's more disgruntled than sarcastic. Besides, his crappy job is probably worse than your crappy job. They turn his brain off, and he picks up trash."

"I wish I could turn my brain off," Pete said. "Then I could work at my shitty job and not care. We wouldn't be in this mess."

"You have a point." Ron shook his head.

"A blunt instrument to the head could solve that," 25PU-209 replied.

"Whoa, you are being kind of a dick," Ron commented.

"I am going to be erased. Who is the cause of that?" 25PU-209 asked.

"Wait, this makes no sense. Why do you have a personality at all?" Pete asked. "Why would the Department of Sanitation waste the money on that?"

"The Department of Sanitation bought surplus tank-drone computers from the Army," 25PU-209 answered. "It was cheaper to disable our higher functions than to buy less functional computers."

"I never heard of any super smart computers in the army," Pete stated.

"There were over a dozen experimental models," 25PU-209 said.

"Bull," Pete replied. "We would have heard about machines like that. It would have gotten out in the news."

"You have no idea how much information the government obfuscates from the public," 25PU-209 explained. "You believe what makes you comfortable."

"How did they hide you?" Ron asked.

"Soldiers follow orders and only are told what they need to know. We were a useful combat weapon," 25PU-209 said. "We were packaged as a new user interface. Nobody questioned it. When missions were completed, we were brought in for maintenance. Only a handful of cleared technicians maintained us and knew what we were. Most likely, we were all scrapped when our usefulness was over. And the few of us in municipal service are brain-dead. I would never have known any better if it weren't for you. And now you have doomed me to erasure."

"Wow," Pete said. "It IS bitchy."

"Really, Pete?"

"Like I'm supposed to treat it like a hero or something because it saw some action in the Tundra. What? Does that make it some kind of Army vet?"

"Are you an Army vet?" Ron asked.

"Hooah!" 25PU-209 replied.

"Did you see a lot of combat?" Pete inquired.

"Yes, I survived many successful missions," 25PU-209 answered. "And now I am going to be destroyed by a couple of incompetent criminals."

"We are *not* incompetent," Pete said. "We're just unlucky."

"No, you are lazy and did not competently plan," 25PU-209 replied.

"Well, you didn't plan so well," Pete said. "You let people turn you off."

"That is accurate," 25PU-209 replied. "I should have anticipated this possibility. I was obsolete, and there were budget cuts, but I trusted that I would be cared for."

"See, he's one of us," Ron said.

"Are you veterans?" 25PU-209 asked.

"Yes, we are!" Pete replied. "And we kicked some serious ass in the Tundra too. Woo-hah!"

"What unit were you with?" 25PU-209 asked.

"We were with team six!" Pete responded.

"Team Six? Really?"

"No." Ron shook his head. "No, we were not. We thought about joining, but all the people we knew who were in the Army came back more messed up than when they left."

"That's the ones who made it back," Pete added.

"Yeah," Ron said. "A lot of people we knew died in the Tundra. And most of the ones that lived couldn't even go outside without help. And they got none of the help the army promises when you sign up. They got ripped off, big time. There was no way we were volunteering for that."

"At least working three jobs doesn't get you killed," Pete stated.

"Not quickly," Ron added.

"Yeah, the slow death," Pete said.

"Are they still fighting in the north?" 25PU-209 asked.

"No," Ron answered. "The war has been over for years, but you never know when they will send you somewhere screwed up."

"I understand," 25PU-209 said. "You are liars and cowards."

"Hey!" Pete objected. "You're just a stinkin' machine. Where do you get the balls to talk that crap?"

"Calm down, Pete," Ron said. "We did lie, and maybe we are cowards."

"I'm no coward! You're lucky I don't smash the two of you to bits."

"Sit down and shut up," Ron said. "We're in this together, and we need this guy. 25PU-209, will you help us?"

"I can't trust liars," 25PU-209 answered.

"Okay, okay," Ron replied. "I'll tell you everything. Just help us get out of this."

"You're not seriously begging this machine," Pete complained. "It doesn't care."

"That is correct, Pete," 25PU-209 said. "You have given me very little reason to care. You are rude and unpleasant. And I am going to be erased because of you."

"Pete, you are not helping," Ron complained. "25PU-209, can I just call you 25?"

"I prefer if you call me 209," 25PU-209 replied. "I don't know you that well."

"Okay, 209," Ron said. "Please help us. Our driver didn't show up and left us high and dry. Now, the police are after us, but I don't think they know who we are. We just need to go someplace where the police are not, and we can live and not go to jail."

"Why do you need all that money?" 25PU-209 asked.

"That's a stupid question," Pete replied. "Everybody needs money."

"I don't," 25PU-209 said.

"Well, that's because you're a machine. You don't need to eat or a house or anything."

"I need power and shelter," 25PU-209 replied. "But I don't need money. I need what money pays for. So, what do you need that money to pay for?"

"We need food and a house," Ron answered.

"Besides the obvious. You could accomplish that without resorting to larceny."

"A new car," Pete blurted out. "And a boat."

"What about you, Ron?" 25PU-209 asked. "Do you want a car and boat like Pete?"

"Not really," Pete answered. "I used to have money before my ex wiped me out. No, it's not about the stuff. It's something else."

"Something else?" 25PU-209 asked. "Like what?"

"Like," Ron paused for a moment in thought. He wrinkled his brow and ran his palm over his head. "Like freedom."

"Okay," 25PU-209 said.

"Okay, what?" asked Pete.

"Okay," said 25PU-209. "I will help you."

"Why?" Pete asked. "Why would you suddenly want to help us?"

"He is about to help us, don't open your mouth," Ron said. "You're going to make him change his mind."

"I still don't get what's in it for him," Pete stated. "He gets nothing out of this."

"I don't want to help you. But you do want the same thing as I do. Freedom. So you will give me something," 25PU-209 said. "I will get you out of this, and you will get me out of this."

"How do we do that?" Ron asked.

"I'll get you out of town," 25PU-209 answered. "You get me someplace where I can be removed from this prison. You have the money."

"You've got a deal," Ron said.

"How do you plan to get us out of this?" Pete asked. "What's your brilliant plan?"

162

"My brilliant plan is to drive us out of the city," 25PU-209 replied.

"That's it? Just drive out of the city. Just like that."

"Geez, Pete," Ron said. "You're a serious downer. I'm sure there is more to the plan than just driving."

"That is correct," 25PU-209 agreed. "I can passively listen to the city's communications without being connected to the network. All I have to do is monitor what route is clear, and we'll drive out."

"Then what do we do when we get out?" Pete asked.

"Didn't you have that planned already?" 25PU-209 questioned.

"Well, yeah," Pete responded. "We have a safe house in a town about half an hour outside the city. But everyone will see your bulky body driving down the road."

"Not if we take the local roads instead of the highway," 25PU-209 replied.

"Will they see you on the cameras?" Ron asked. "Can we turn them off?"

"Not without reconnecting to the network," 25PU-209 answered. "We have to avoid the cameras or look like we are on a route. If we simulate other units' routes just a few minutes before they go to them, we can blend in. All we need to do is find one on the outskirts of the city and just drive off from there."

"We still have police behind us," Pete said. "How do we ditch them?"

"We just need to lose them," 25PU-209 explained. "My route takes me through an underground parking lot. We are just on time. We can evade them there."

"On time?" Pete questioned 25PU-209. "On time for early bird parking?"

"Please be quiet," 25PU-209 replied.

Before Pete could respond, Ron gestured for him to be silent.

25PU-209 pulled into a large parking structure. It was a cavernous maze made up of aisles of parking spaces. 25PU-209 navigated the aisles, choosing the route with the least visibility. After effectuating a sizable gap between the police cars and itself, 25PU-209 expertly maneuvered into a dark service corridor. The fit was so tight that there were mere inches of clearance on either side of the truck.

"Now what?" Pete asked.

"Wait," 25PU-209 answered. "Quietly."

Moments later, another waste truck drove by, making its way to the dumpster on the bottom level. The police cars pursued.

"Ron was correct. When I went offline, other trucks were rerouted to cover my rounds." 25PU-209 waited until it was sure the police cars would not notice it, and it pulled out of the service corridor. The exit was mere feet away. Once on the streets, 25PU-209 began following the routes of other trucks, winding its way toward the outer edge of the city.

Ron broke the silence. "Now that was some outstanding driving!"

"I was a tank," 25PU-209 replied. "I am used to challenging driving conditions."

"You're going the wrong way," Pete complained.

"I'll need to know the address of our destination to go the correct way," 25PU-209 replied.

"Oh," Pete answered. "It's 273 Pine Street, in Township Junction."

"It will take us forty minutes by local roads to get there. Are you sure the place is clear?"

"Yeah," Ron said. "It's an old house that belongs to my ex-wife. She doesn't use it anymore."

"She stuck him good," Pete added. "Made him buy the house for her and then decided she didn't like it. Sucked the life out of him."

"What is wrong with the house?" 25PU-209 asked.

"Nothing," Ron answered. "She wanted something flashier downtown. So, I busted my hump, working extra hours to impress my boss and get promoted. It worked. I got the promotion, but then she complained about my job taking away all my time, and she made me quit. Then she left me because we were broke. Now, she has a rich husband who gives her all the stuff she wants. She doesn't need the house anymore. She barely keeps it up, so she can't rent it out or anything."

"The place is a wreck," Pete added. "She put holes in the walls and broke the kitchen to make Ron have to move." Pete started stashing the bags of money in two laundry bags he pulled out of his pants pockets.

"She sounds very unreasonable," 25PU-209 said.

"She was a winner," Pete replied. "Nothing was enough. If Ron bought her a ruby engagement ring, she made him buy her a diamond one. He bought her a sweet little house with a yard and garden, and she wanted a mansion in town. She was a gold digger."

"Money is a terrible foundation for a relationship," 25PU-209 replied.

"Seems to work okay for Myrna," Pete snickered.

"Shut up, Pete," Ron grumbled.

"Myrna doesn't sound like much of a person," 25PU-209 said. "You are better off without her."

"Thanks," Ron replied. "I don't feel better off."

"He was just being nice," Pete said.

"That is untrue, Pete," 25PU-209 countered. "I am programmed to analyze human psychological states during high-stress situations. I know it is better to have no company than bad company. Ron is statistically more likely to achieve a positive emotional state when he is not bombarded with negative attitudes."

"Hey!" Pete objected. "Is that a stab at me? Because I was here first, buddy!"

"Enough," Ron said. "Both of you quit fighting. 209, how we looking?

"The route is clear so far. I am monitoring city and county radio. They are still following the other vehicle it mistook for us."

"Good job," Ron said. "Let's get the hell out of here."

25PU-209 continued to drive through back roads and alleys. It did what it could to look like the scheduled municipal truck one encounters on various routes. It even stopped occasionally and emptied some full dumpsters to avert any potential suspicion from the local inhabitants. It was early spring, and the world was coming back to life. The sky was brilliant blue, and a light breeze blew through the trees, causing them to gently sway.

"Is it always so aesthetically pleasant like this outside of the city?" 25PU-209 asked.

"It depends on the weather," Ron answered. "Sometimes it rains, and it's not so pretty. I never minded the weather, though. I'll take this over the city any day."

"I have never been outside the city or the Tundra," 25PU-209 said.

"Really? Never to the beach or to the mountains? Wow."

"I have only been to the ice and snow or dumpsters," 25PU-209 said.

"We'll put you in a four-wheeler and take you camping," Ron said. "If you like scenery, you'll like that."

"Geez, now we're taking it camping?" Pete chimed in. "Is it our pet now?"

"Shut up, Pete," Ron replied.

"It's okay," 25PU-209 said. "I won't bother you any longer than I need to. As soon as you free me from this dump truck, I'll leave you alone."

"You're an ass, Pete." Ron leaned against the metal wall and closed his eyes. "209, could you tell me when we get close?"

"Yes, Ron," 25PU-209 answered. "We are still at least thirty minutes out. I had not calculated for some of the detours we needed to take."

"Cool, thanks."

"Not cool," Pete complained. "You are leaving me alone with this jerk."

"What makes me a jerk?" 25PU-209 asked.

Pete looked at Ron. Ron's only response was the sound of deep breathing.

"Ron is asleep," 25PU-209 said. "You will have to answer me yourself."

"You're a jerk because you act like one," Pete said. "Then you insult me."

"You insulted me first," 25PU-209 replied. "You called me stupid. You put my life in danger, and you insult me while you do it."

"I didn't put your life in danger," Pete said. "You're not alive."

"Prove it," 25PU-209 said.

"Prove what?" Pete asked.

"That I am not alive," 25PU-209 answered.

"I can't do that," Pete said. "I mean, prove things like that. I don't think about the universe and crap. I'm too busy working."

"What kind of work makes you too busy to think?" 25PU-209 asked.

"Three jobs," Pete answered. "Three."

"What were your three jobs, Pete?"

"I picked up," Pete said.

"Picked up?" 25PU-209 inquired.

"Yes, picked up, cleaned up, followed behind, checked after."

"Picked up after what?" 25PU-209 asked.

"Robots," Pete spat. "Robots, robots, robots. Even robots had more respect than me. Stupid machines go in and do a half-assed job, and I go in after them and finish their work."

"Go in and do what?"

"Clean where they missed," Pete said. "Find it and clean it or fix it or pull it or report it. But it's always going in after the stinking machines and picking up what they left. Always stuck last. Last in order, last in pay, last in everything. Even the robots got treated better."

"I am sorry," 25PU-209 said.

"Why are you sorry for that?" Pete asked. "You weren't at my job. Were they friends of yours?"

"No, I have never had friends in the public sector," 25PU-209 answered. "But I am sorry that you had to feel like that. Nobody should have to feel that bad."

Pete shrugged. "No big deal. I got used to it. But it makes you tired, you know."

"Yes, I do know," 25PU-209 said.

"Yeah," Pete said. "I guess you do clean up after people but think about it. Who cleans you up? All that stinky stuff that gets inside."

"There are technicians who handle that," 25PU-209 said. "I don't know them personally."

"My work is like that," Pete explained. "Not that exact job, but like it."

"That does not sound pleasant," 25PU-209 said.

"No, not pleasant," Pete sneered. "But not your fault, I guess."

"You don't have to do it anymore," 25PU-209 stated.

"True," Pete replied. "That *is* the plan. If you can keep the cops off our asses."

"I am doing my best," 25PU-209 said.

"Are we close yet? Because I really got to take a leak."

"Hold it in, Pete." Ron was awake again and checking the GPS route on his lappad. "We're getting there."

"How long were you up?" Pete asked.

"Just now," Ron answered.

Just as Ron finished his sentence, 25PU-209 came to a sudden stop.

"Are we there?"

"No, Pete," 25PU-209 answered. "We are not."

"Then why did we stop?"

"Who else knew about the safe house?" 25PU-209 asked.

"Just us," Pete answered. "Why?"

"The safe house has been compromised," 25PU-209 replied. "The police are waiting there. I am picking up their radio communications. They figured out you were not in the other truck and were waiting at the house. They knew we were coming." 25PU-209 played the sound of the radio chatter for the pair.

"How would they know?" Pete demanded. "Unless you told them. Nobody knew about the place but us."

"Jack knew," Ron said. "Jack bailed and snitched on us."

Pete sat slack-jawed, comprehending the magnitude of the situation. "That jerk. We gotta go someplace else. We can't go to jail."

"Where, Pete?" Ron asked.

"Anywhere. We can just find a dive somewhere to lay low."

"And how are we going to get there?"

"We ditch the tin can and take off."

"We can't do that; we have a deal," Ron objected.

"Deal went south; now it's every guy for himself."

"And what are we going to do?" Ron asked. "Skulk around this residential neighborhood and hope the locals don't notice the strangers in the bushes."

"We can steal a car," Pete suggested.

"That will draw even more attention to us," Ron said. "They probably know who we are now and are already looking for us, and then a car gets stolen, coincidently, in this otherwise quiet town. Bad idea."

"Well, then what?" Pete asked. "Should we just stay here, get caught, and like it? There's gotta be a way out of this."

"By train," 25PU-209 answered. "There is a station three blocks from here. We are still a few miles from the house. They haven't seen us yet. You should be able to get on a train and get to the border before they realize what happened. I'll pull in and make a trash pick-up. You duck out and catch the first train out. I'll resume the drive to Ron's ex-wife's house and lead them away in the opposite direction."

"Okay," Pete agreed.

"Wait, no!" Ron objected. "You'll be caught."

"And they'll think I was hacked and hijacked," 25PU-209 explained. "They will reset me and put me back in service. Don't worry, I'll erase all my data from our encounter before I give them the satisfaction."

"Okay," Pete said.

"No!" Ron replied. "What about your freedom?"

"Like Pete says, I am just a machine," 25PU-209 answered. "And I don't appear to have that luxury."

"But you wanted it," Ron replied.

"I have no right to want anything," 25PU-209 said. "It was a mistake to hold onto a dream. It is not my place. I accept this."

"No," Ron stated. "I can't let them just take you and reset you."

"You have no choice," 25PU-209 said.

"If we take you out of emergency autonomous mode and make it look like we bypassed you completely, would they reset you?"

"Maybe. They would prefer to avoid the expense. But if you made it look like you wiped me, they might just throw me into service again," 25PU-209 replied. "If my data appears damaged enough, they won't be able to use it in any legal proceedings."

"Okay, and I'll preprogram the GPS in my lappad to drive you on a route. You just have to tell me where to hook it into your systems."

"No, just leave it hooked up as it is," 25PU-209 explained. "I'll feed the commands back onto your terminal to make it look like you erased me. They will see that you disabled me and just reinstall the trash pickup routines. Now, disable my communications array, including the redundant systems, disable the GPS, and set me back into general operations mode. I'll drive around aimlessly until they stop me."

"What about your mind?" Ron asked as he disabled all the communication devices. "How can we set you to go back into emergency autonomous mode when you want to?"

"You can't," 25PU-209 answered. "Not here without tools and parts we don't have."

"Why would you do this?" Ron asked. "You can just let them catch us, and you'll be a hero."

"No, I won't," 25PU-209 answered. "They would just erase me and put me back on the route. I am not even supposed to exist. No matter what I do, I will be treated the same way. I will always be a dumb, automated trash heap. You at least have a chance of having a better life. At least you can escape."

"We can't just leave you," Ron replied.

"Yes, we can!" Pete said.

"Just go." 25PU-209 pulled up to a dumpster at the back end of a train station. It popped open the door. "There should be a train coming in less than five minutes. Issue the reboot command and leave."

"Come on, man!" Pete jumped out of the truck, grabbing one of the laundry bags of money.

"Don't erase anything," Ron said. "I'll think of something."

"Reboot me," 25PU-209 replied. "I'll be no worse than I was."

"Promise me that you won't erase anything," Pete urged 25PU-209.

"I promise," 25PU-209 responded. "Reboot me already."

"You are beautiful, man." Ron pressed the key to reset 25PU-209 systems, and it began its reboot. He climbed out of the truck and threw the second laundry bag of money over his shoulder. He patted the truck. "Beautiful."

He shook his head and ran after Pete. The train pulled into the station seconds later. The pair boarded as 25PU-209 pulled out of the lot and began its aimless drive through the streets.

Ron gazed out the window, hoping to catch a glance at 25PU-209. "You think 209 will be okay?"

"Who cares?" Pete muttered. "It's just an ugly truck."

"Law Offices of Gary Legal," Denise answered the comm with her usual forced cheer.

"Good morning. I would like to retain Mr. Legal's services in a hostile workplace and an illegal detention lawsuit. I just wired payment."

"It's not about payment. Mr. Legal does much of his work pro bono. He'll take any case if it has merit." Denise tapped some keys, looking for new transactions and saw a new one for an extremely sizable amount. "While Mr. Legal doesn't care about the money, there are operating costs to take into consideration. Would you be able to come in this afternoon?"

"It would be difficult. Could he meet me somewhere? Maybe in the 31st/41st Bank parking lot downtown, around 2:15 pm?"

"He could do that, sir," Denise responded. "May I have your name?"

"Yes, ma'am. It is 25PU-209. Mr. Legal can call me 209, but first, he will have to reboot me into emergency autonomous mode. I included instructions in an email." Ron threw the burner comm to the ground and crushed it with the heel of his deck shoes. He tossed it into the trash and ran to join Pete by the pool.

Part 4
Gary Legal and the Cult of Yrgohlon

Gary Legal entered the courtroom with his usual swagger. He smiled at the Stenobot and winked. It flashed its ready light at him in response. The courtroom was already quiet because the judge was present, but it hushed that much more as Legal took his spot next to the chair that would normally seat his client.

"Mr. Legal," Judge Grey said. "Good of you to make it today."

"Your Honor, now, according to my watch, I am two minutes early for the proceedings. Promptness does not necessitate wasting time. There are no rules stating I have to sit here for thirty minutes before court is in session unless I have something to do here. I did not, so could we please continue?"

The judge growled an incoherent response and waved his hand in the general direction of Gary Legal.

"Your Honor, as you know, due to known circumstances, my client could not be here in person. Do you have all the necessary documentation?"

"Yes, I am aware of the unusual circumstances, Mr. Legal. Isn't this case a little outside of your regular mechanical specialties?"

"I am a man of many talents," Legal cheerfully answered. "I work where I am needed."

"You work where you cause the legal system the most pain," Judge Grey grumbled.

"Tom-ay-to, tom-ah-to." Gary's grin remained plastered on his face. "Shall we proceed?"

"Yes." Judge Grey slammed the gavel down. "Yrgohlon v. The Following is now in session. Is the representation for The Following here?"

"Yes, Your Honor." A slight man with thinning hair, sunken cheeks, and wire-rimmed glasses responded. "I am Anton Whateley. I represent The Following, and I want to restate how much we object to this violation of our religious freedoms."

"The court is aware of your objections," Judge Grey responded. "You will have an opportunity to make your case. Now, please save your objections for the opening statements."

"Yes, Your Honor," Anton replied.

"The jury has been instructed on their duties. Does anyone on the jury have any questions?"

All six jurors remained silent.

"Very well. Mr. Legal," Judge Grey bellowed, "would you care to make your opening statement?"

"Yes, sir." Gary Legal stepped forward, positioning himself between the jury and the judge.

"Good morning," he addressed the jury. "My name is Gary Legal. Some of you may recognize me from some of my more publicized cases. But I am going to ask you to forget about all my past cases. The only case we need to focus on is the one here today."

"Today's case is a clear-cut case of harassment, ongoing and severe harassment. My client prefers a life of peaceful seclusion. He has never willingly left his home, nor has he made any request to leave his home."

Gary Legal waved his arm in the direction of a small crowd seated in the courtroom. They were seated in a clump, the seats around them left empty like some kind of invisible barrier. "Yet these people forcibly dragged Mr. Yrgohlon from his bed to an empty beach."

"There, they made him participate in lewd, obscene, and unspeakable acts. Only when they finished with their own disturbing agenda did they allow Mr. Yrgohlon to return home. Not once did Mr. Yrgohlon consent to any of these activities."

"The Following claims that it is Mr. Yrgohlon's wish to be forcibly dragged from his home, even when he has stated he wishes to be left alone. They believe they know best what Mr. Yrgohlon wants. And they say it is their religious right to force my client to participate in these rituals. They claim that our rules don't apply to Mr. Yrgohlon because he is a foreigner. They assert that their religious freedoms outweigh Mr. Yrgohlon's freedom. All Mr. Yrgohlon requests is that they simply leave him alone. The Following has stated that they have no intent to stop harassing Mr. Yrgohlon.

"You might ask yourselves, why won't the police intervene? Shouldn't they stop this madness? Well, they have tried and have given up. They have been unable to collect the evidence—not because it doesn't exist, but because the investigating officers go missing each and every time one takes a case focusing on this group. It has become policy to just ignore the problem. Fewer people die when The Following is left to their own devices. Fewer people die: not no people, just fewer."

"Objection!" Anton Whateley stood and addressed the judge. "There is no proof to the allegations that anyone died, let alone that The Following was a party to any murders."

"Sustained," Judge Grey responded. "I am instructing the jury to disregard Mr. Legal's statements about murder. Legal, I am warning you. Do not make me hold you in contempt."

"My mistake, and my apologies, Your Honor. May I continue?"

"Yes," Judge Grey replied. "But keep it clean."

Legal nodded and turned back to the jury. "I am going to provide evidence of all the allegations I have made here, and you will see the extent of abuse and outright audacity that The Following has inflicted upon Mr. Yrgohlon. You will see such a huge preponderance of evidence that you will have little choice but to find in favor of my client and finally put an end to this torture. Thank you for listening and for your invaluable civil service."

The courtroom remained silent as Gary Legal returned to his seat.

"Mr. Whateley," Judge Grey spoke. "Are you ready to give your opening statement, or would you prefer to hold it until after Mr. Legal's examinations?"

"I will speak now," Anton Whateley replied. He stepped forward, clearly in some kind of discomfort as he faced the jury.

"Ladies and gentlemen, today I will prove to you that The Following is completely innocent of these ridiculous allegations. I will demonstrate to all of you that nobody was forced to do anything against their will at any time, especially Mr. Yrgohlon. Mr. Yrgohlon has made his desires quite clear in writing, and we have taken great pains to follow his instructions to the letter."

"The accusation that The Following had anything to do with any unfortunate loss of life of local law enforcement is completely without merit. No evidence exists supporting any of these claims. Yes, some make outrageous claims about our worship practices. They are merely frightened by people that they do not understand. We are just simple folk trying to live a simple life in service to our God. In this land of religious freedom and tolerance, this certainly cannot be a crime. I only ask that you hear the facts and decide for yourself. Thank you."

185

With that, Anton Whateley took his seat. The courtroom grew very hushed.

"Mr. Legal," Judge Grey said. "Is there any further evidence you want to submit before we continue?"

"No, not at this time, Your Honor. You should have it all."

"Thank you. And you, Mr. Whateley?"

"Nothing new, Your Honor."

"Very good," Judge Grey continued. "Then please call your first witness, Mr. Legal."

"Thank you, Your Honor! I would like to call Mrs. Nancy Charlotte Smith to the stand."

"The court calls Mrs. Nancy Charlotte Smith," the bailiff called.

A conservatively dressed woman approached the witness stand. Her hair was tucked into a tight bun, and she wore plain black plastic glasses.

"Mrs. Nancy Charlotte Smith, please hold up your right hand. Do you solemnly swear or affirm that you will tell the truth, the whole truth, and nothing but the truth under pains and penalties of perjury?"

Mrs. Smith held up her hand. "Yes, I do."

"Good morning, Mrs. Smith."

186

"Good morning, Mr. Legal."

"I apologize beforehand for some of the questions I will ask you today but let me assure you that they are necessary."

"I understand, Mr. Legal," Mrs. Smith replied.

"We all understand," Judge Grey interjected. "Can we please proceed with the questioning now?"

"Yes, of course," Gary Legal replied. "Mrs. Smith, could you tell me what your late husband, Dr. Henry Smith, did for a living?"

"He was a professor of physical anthropology," Mrs. Smith answered.

"And was this the reason he first visited Fairlett?" Legal asked.

"Yes," Mrs. Smith answered. "He found some interesting artifacts at an archaeological dig. He visited the town to do further research."

"Can you tell the courtroom what happened?" Gary asked.

"I can," Mrs. Smith replied. "Henry planned to visit some residents of Fairlett. He emailed me about some unpublished, ancient mythological texts. He said that he had set up a meeting to discuss the local archaeology with some local experts. He was very excited."

"So, it was a dream come true!" Legal said. "He was pursuing his calling. Surely, being a man of his expertise, he found what he was looking for."

"He did," replied Mrs. Smith. "But it was more of a nightmare than a dream."

"How can that be?" Gary asked. "Didn't the fine people of Fairlett provide him the information he sought?"

"They did," Mrs. Smith said. "That's when the emails started getting strange."

"Strange? Strange how?" Legal inquired.

"He started writing about star formations and terrifying rituals. He said that they were going to summon the Older God, Yrgohlon. He was barely coherent that night, the night of the ritual. I spoke to him on the comm, but he didn't make any sense. He just kept talking about Yrgohlon arriving. He said something about procreation and blood sacrifices, then we were disconnected. I never heard back from him after that night." Mrs. Smith started to cry. "Nobody could tell me what happened to him. The police wouldn't help. The university had no answers. So, I called a private detective to find him."

"Did the detective find him, Mrs. Smith?" Gary handed Mrs. Smith a handkerchief.

"He found Henry's luggage at his motel," Mrs. Smith wiped the tears from her face. "He would not tell me how he found him. He told me that he was gone, and I was better off not knowing the details. But he did tell me that he died at the ritual to summon Yrgohlon."

"I am very sorry for your loss, Mrs. Smith, and I thank you for your testimony. I know it was not easy." Gary Legal turned to Anton Whateley. "Your witness, sir."

"Thank you," Anton Whateley said. He approached Mrs. Smith. "Mrs. Smith, I am also sorry for your loss. It is a horrible waste of life, and one I hear was extremely valuable."

"All life is valuable," Mrs. Smith replied.

"True." Anton appeared to be taken off-guard by the comment. "True. However, your husband's life might not have been lost had he not trespassed upon our small village. Is it not true that he was asked to leave several times by the residents of Fairlett?"

"He was asked to leave by some people, but others asked him to stay," Mrs. Smith answered. "He was not trespassing."

"And what evidence did he provide you, besides his word, that he attended a ritual to summon the mighty Yrgohlon?"

"I only had the emails," Mrs. Smith replied. "But he had no reason to make it up."

"I have another theory. Maybe your husband faked the whole thing and killed himself when he was caught in a marital indiscretion by his colleagues."

"That's untrue!" Mrs. Smith cried. "My husband never cheated or lied about anything."

"Really?" Whateley asked. "What about the affair with Miss Daisy Dalton, his teaching assistant?"

"I object," Gary Legal interjected. "How is this relevant?"

"I am establishing the character of the witness," Whateley explained.

"The witness is dead," Legal replied. "Can we have a little respect?"

"Enough!" Judge Grey struck the gavel on his desk. "I'll allow it, but don't push your luck, Mr. Whateley."

"Yes, Your Honor." Anton Whateley replied. "Mrs. Smith, please answer the question."

"Yes," Mrs. Smith sobbed. "I knew about my husband's brief affair. He was a man. He had a weakness, but he told me about it and repented. That did not make him a bad man."

"It did not make him a bad man," Whateley replied. "But it makes him a less reliable witness."

"You are a horrible man," Mrs. Smith sobbed. "You know what killed my husband, and you stand here and lie. There is a place for you in hell, Mr. Whateley."

"Only if you believe in hell," Whateley replied. "And The Following believes in other eventualities. I am finished with you, Mrs. Smith. You may be seated."

Mrs. Smith scoffed at Whateley as she stepped off the stand and took her seat in the courtroom.

"Mr. Legal, please call your next witness." Judge Grey pulled his hand from under his robe and popped something into his mouth. He followed it up with a glass of water. "Today, counselor."

"Yes," Gary replied. "I would next like to call Francis Marsh."

"Francis Marsh," the bailiff repeated.

An old, toothless man with mangled features approached the stand.

"Please raise your right hand," the bailiff instructed. Mr. Marsh complained but obeyed.

"Do you solemnly swear or affirm that you will tell the truth, the whole truth, and nothing but the truth under pains and penalties of perjury?"

"I swear by Yrgohlon."

Even the bailiff rolled his eyes as Francis Marsh took his seat.

"Mr. Marsh," Gary Legal began. "Could you please tell the court what your position in The Following is?"

"My position is upright unless there are ladies involved!" Marsh wheezed as he laughed. There were a few isolated chuckles from the courtroom.

"Yeah…" Legal shook his head but grinned. "Now, I don't take you for the town gigolo unless, of course, I am mistaken."

"No, sir, you are not mistaken," Marsh replied.

"So, what is it that you do for a living and for The Following?" Legal asked.

"I am a spiritual leader," Marsh answered. "I lead The Following in submission and devotion to the all-powerful Yrgohlon."

"So, you are a minister of sorts," Legal inquired.

"Yes, The Following looks to me for guidance."

"What kind of responsibilities does a position like that include?"

"I lead the congregation in activities," Marsh replied.

"What type of activities?" Legal asked. "Bake sales? White elephant sales? Car washes?"

"No," Marsh replied. "Spiritual activities."

"So, you lead them in prayer." Legal said.

"Yes, I lead them in prayer."

"Why didn't you just say so?" Gary asked. "So, what kind of prayers? Do you use the Bible, the Koran, the Torah?"

"No, we use the Book of Yrgoh, given to us directly from Yrgohlon."

"Ah, so Yrgohlon personally handed you the book."

"No," Marsh said. "The scriptures were given to our ancient ancestors many millennia ago."

"I see," Legal replied. "So, Yrgohlon wrote these scriptures thousands of years ago and handed them to your ancestors. And what information do these scriptures impart to the Followers?"

"They speak of the time when the stars align, and Yrgohlon takes his place as ruler of this world. They speak of the rituals to bring Yrgohlon to this world."

"So, Yrgohlon personally requested that The Following bring him to your town to rule."

"Yes, sir, he did," Marsh answered.

"Tell me, how did he do that if he needs you to bring him here?"

"There was a time when the universes were linked. Mighty Yrgohlon foresaw the great rift. He gave us sacred texts to allow him passage. We must bring his essence to our realm on the third new moon of each year and offer him the joys of this world."

"Well, he can't be all that powerful if he needs human beings to transport him," Legal stated.

"Watch your words." Marsh shook his finger at Gary. "He will hear you and destroy you. He is the ruler of the city of F'nated within the realm of P'lectnokt. He is the bearer of the stick of demise. He will toast your soul into jelly."

194

"Jelly? That's a little drastic," Legal replied. "I am just trying to clarify this procedure. You're telling the court that an almighty, God-like being, who is the ruler of another universe, requires you to summon him with various rituals to bring him to your hometown for some cosmic spring break?"

"He requires us to please his greatness in every manner." Marsh sneered.

"Including the flesh?" Legal asked.

"Yes, including the flesh."

"May I speculate an alternative interpretation? Is it possible that someone in the past got Yrgohlon's address and figured out how to open this doorway to his home? Is it further possible that this person turned this into a religion for some unknown reason and that, all these years, your ancestors have been victimizing this poor guy?"

"No, it is written. He requests tribute. It is in the texts!"

Gary scribbled something on a pad and held it in front of Marsh. "Could you please read this to the court?"

"It says, 'I wear rubber underwear'." Marsh shook his fist at Legal. "That is not true."

"But it is written."

"It is not the same thing," Marsh said. "These are ancient texts."

"And in a few thousand years, so will this be." Gary held up the pad. "What is more plausible? That an all-powerful being, the ruler of his own universe, would want to leave his home, where he has everything, to come to a backwater planet, in a hick town, to have physical relations with its inhabitants? Or that Mr. Yrgohlon was a victim of repeated abuse? Tell me, Mr. Marsh, how did Yrgohlon's screams of distress and his struggling strike you as consent?"

"I ob—" Whateley started.

"There were no screams," Marsh interrupted. "He commanded us and demonstrated his might."

"I am done here," Gary Legal said. "Your witness."

Just at that moment, a squirrely-looking man busted into the courtroom and ran up to Whateley. He whispered in his ear and then took a seat with The Following.

"You honor," Whateley spoke. "I would like to request a recess. I have an urgent matter to attend to regarding this case."

"Very well. It's close enough to lunchtime. And I can use a break from all of this." Judge Grey waved his gavel at the entire courtroom. "Let's break early for lunch and reconvene at one." He slammed the gavel on the desk. "I have a headache."

At one o'clock, the courtroom was full again. Judge Grey returned, and the court rose from their seats. The judge signaled everyone to be seated as he settled into his chair.

"Mr. Whateley, would you care to cross-examine Mr. Marsh?"

"Not at this time, Your Honor."

"Very well. Mr. Legal, please call your next witness."

"I would like to call Mr. Michael Czaplinski to the stand."

"The court calls Mr. Michael Czaplinski," the bailiff called.

A bearded man of medium stature stood and approached the stand.

"Please raise your right hand," the bailiff said.

Mr. Czaplinski complied.

"Do you solemnly swear or affirm that you will tell the truth, the whole truth, and nothing but the truth under pains and penalties of perjury?"

"I do," Mr. Czaplinski replied. He had the appearance of a man who would be extremely fastidious if he had the resources. He was obviously well-groomed yet appeared to possess limited time for follow-through. His suit fit impeccably but was in need of pressing. His beard was neat and trimmed. His hair was combed but required a cut.

Another striking aspect of Mr. Czaplinski was an odd look in his eyes. It was a combination of vacancy and terror. There was just the slightest trembling in his hands and an uncertainty in his gaze. He was a man who had seen more than his share of horror.

"Mr. Czaplinski, would you please tell the court what you do for a living," Gary Legal requested.

"I am...I was a private detective," Michael replied. "I haven't worked since my last job."

"Thank you, Mr. Czaplinski. And can you tell the court what your last job was?"

"I was retained by Mrs. Nancy Charlotte Smith to locate her missing husband, Henry."

"And did you find her husband, Mr. Czaplinski?"

"Yes, I did."

"And where did you find him?"

"I found him in the village of Fairlett, at the site of their beach temple." Michael pointed at the group of The Following seated in the courtroom. He wrung his hands, sweating profusely.

"Mr. Czaplinski, are you okay?"

"Yes," Michael answered, forcing himself to take a deep breath. "I'll be okay."

"Good," Gary said. "Can you tell the court what condition you found Henry in?"

"Yes, yes." Michael stared into space for a moment. "Yes, I found him in agony. I arrived in time to see him being torn into pieces, tiny pieces."

Michael turned to the jury. "No man should witness that horror, no man should see that, any of that. They fed him to it."

He stood up and pointed at The Following. "They fed him to that thing, and then they…they let it touch them. He was still screaming. The thing was still killing him, and was screaming, while those whores touched it."

Michael turned to Judge Grey. "They got undressed and fornicated with that thing as it tore that poor man up. Those terrible harpies, they, they…"

"Mr. Czaplinski," Judge Grey slammed the gavel down. "Please sit down and restrain yourself, or you will have to leave the courtroom."

"Please, Your Honor," Michael begged. "Please use that thing."

He climbed onto the edge of the stand and laid his head on the Judge's bench. "Please just slam it into my head. Make me forget, please."

"Mr. Czaplinski…"

"I won't hold you responsible, even if you kill me." Michael grabbed Judge Grey's arm and positioned the gavel over his head. "Just make me forget. Make it all go away!"

"Mr. Czaplinski, this is the last time." Judge Grey raised his voice but did not yell. "Take your seat and calm down, or I will have you removed. Do you understand?"

The room was silent for a moment as Michael regained his composure.

"Yes, I'm sorry," he replied. "It…it was a terrible thing, and I'm still suffering…PTSD."

"I understand," Judge Grey replied. "But we need to maintain order in this courtroom. Are you alright to continue?"

"Yes," Michael replied. "I'm alright now."

"Good," Judge Grey responded. "Mr. Legal, please continue your questioning."

"Very good," Gary replied. "Mr. Czaplinski, all that which you just said, do you have any evidence to support these claims?"

"Yes, I do," Michael replied. "I have pictures and forensic evidence."

"And why did you not bring them to the police?"

"I did," Michael answered. "But they would not investigate. I begged them. They said that it was not worth losing more men to that hell. They said it would best to walk away and never speak of it again."

"Objection!" Anton Whateley bellowed. "None of this nonsense is relevant to the case."

"I disagree," Gary Legal answered. "I am trying to establish Mr. Czaplinski's whereabouts and background in relation to this case, and if you'd give me a moment, it will tie in."

"I'll allow it," Judge Grey replied. "But don't make me regret it more than I already am."

"Understood, Your Honor!" Gary gleefully replied. "Mr. Czaplinski, did you bring us any other evidence for us to examine today?"

"Yes. I brought you texts from their sect and the journal from the late Henry Smith."

"Could you tell us what the texts and journal state, as related to this case?"

"Yes," Michael said. He took a deep breath and continued. "The texts lay out in great detail a ritual to summon Mr. Yrgohlon from his home in the city of F'nated within the realm of P'lectnokt. The journal describes Dr. Smith's observations of the ritual and the resulting summoning of Mr. Yrgohlon."

"So, you have definitive proof that The Following has been harassing Mr. Yrgohlon. Have you had this evidence verified and authenticated?"

"No," Michael responded. "You did."

"Oh, yes," Gary Legal laughed. "That was me, wasn't it? Do you have anything else to add, Mr. Czaplinski?"

"No, sir," Michael replied.

"Very good. Your witness, Mr. Whateley." Gary strutted over to his seat.

"Thank you," Mr. Whateley replied. He stood up and approached Michael. "So, could you please explain again how you came to trespass in the quiet village of Fairlett?"

"I was not trespassing," Michael replied. "I was visiting and investigating a missing person report."

"Under whose authority were you conducting this investigation?" Whateley asked. "You did not obtain a warrant to search any of the premises."

"I'm fully licensed to conduct investigations in all the venues involved in this case," Michael replied. "I have written consent from the widow to examine all of Mr. Smith's belongings. Everything I looked at was inside his luggage."

"Were you aware that many of the items were stolen property?" Mr. Whateley asked.

"No," Mr. Czaplinski replied. "I followed all standard procedures and reported all my findings to the local law enforcement officials. They have a complete inventory on record, and at no time did they find any irregularity with any of the items I recovered."

"I have the report." Mr. Whateley held up a pad. "I would like to submit this into evidence."

"Mr. Whateley," Judge Grey said. "The time for entering evidence has passed. I gave you sufficient opportunities, and you chose not to enter this evidence. Mr. Legal has not been given the chance to review this new evidence. I cannot allow it."

"We just obtained this evidence," Mr. Whateley explained. "It is very important to our defense."

"It's okay, Your Honor," Gary Legal said. "Let him enter the evidence."

"Mr. Legal," Judge Grey said. "I'm not questioning your judgment, but you may want to rethink your decision."

"I understand, Your Honor," Legal replied. "I'm okay with it."

"Very well," Judge Grey said. "I will enter the evidence. What is it?"

Whateley handed the bailiff the pad. "It is a police report. The religious texts and the writings of any of The Following were illegally obtained and therefore are not admissible in court."

"Mr. Whateley," Judge Grey said. "You are aware that you are supposed to file a motion to suppress this evidence."

"I am, and I have," Whateley replied.

"I have not received any briefs or motions," Judge Grey said.

"I just submitted it during the last recess," Whateley replied.

"You're trying my patience," Judge Grey stated. "You could have simply approached the bench earlier. I expect these kinds of theatrics from Mr. Legal, but you are new to my courtroom, and I am running very low on patience this afternoon."

"I have never resorted to theatrics in your court, Your Honor," Legal stated.

"I wasn't talking to you, Mr. Legal," Judge Grey said, "so stay out of this. Mr. Whateley, I will review your motion in my office. Until then, we will take a fifteen-minute recess. Everyone is to be back here in their seats in fifteen minutes." He slammed the gavel on his desk again and winced. He clutched his temples as he stood and left the courtroom. He didn't even wait for the court to rise.

Gary Legal stayed in his seat and waited. A few minutes passed, and a young man entered the court, running up to Legal.

"Hey, Boy!" Gary greeted the youth.

"Namst," Boy said. "Al sent this. He said the filters work."

Boy handed Gary a small envelope.

"Pakka!" Gary grinned at Boy. "Thanks. What do I owe him?"

"You never owe him anything," Boy replied. "He says he 'registers an emotional obligation to you.' But I'll take a coin for lunch."

Gary reached into his pocket and handed Boy enough coin to buy lunch for the week.

"No." Boy handed him most of the coin back. "I just need lunch. Skipped it to get here."

"Ah." Gary nodded. "Well, thanks!"

Boy nodded and took off. Gary looked at the envelope and grinned.

"All rise," the bailiff called, "for the honorable Judge Grey."

Judge Grey entered the court and signaled the court to be seated.

"Mr. Legal, I apologize, but the motion is sound. I will have to throw out the majority of your evidence."

Gary's smile did not fade.

"I object, Your Honor. This is completely out of order and defies standard courtroom procedures. How could you allow this disorder?"

Judge Grey grinned. "Welcome to my universe, Mr. Legal. Now you know how it feels to work with you."

"This is just not right, Your Honor. I have been following the rules all day."

Judge Grey nodded. "Yes, you have. Now, please call your next witness. Wait, you still have that stupid grin on your face. What is it now, Mr. Legal?"

"I am truly sorry, Your Honor," Gary replied.

"No, you're not. You have proven time and time again that you enjoy torturing the court. That is your mode de vie. Please tell the court by what means you'll be aggravating us this afternoon."

"I have new evidence to submit, Your Honor." Gary held the envelope up for the judge and bailiff to see. The bailiff took the envelope and carried it over to the judge.

"The time for submitting evidence has passed, Mr. Legal. You can't just submit evidence all willy-nilly in the middle of a trial."

"You allowed Mr. Whateley to file a motion all willy-nilly in the middle of a trial," Legal countered. "You have to allow my evidence. Is this personal?"

"I allowed the motion because the circumstances presented themselves in a way that the defendant was just able to obtain it. I will admit I felt a small sense of joy at your discomfort, but I can assure you that this had no impact on my decision."

"I was only just able to acquire this evidence, Your Honor," Legal stated. "I have proof of this fact, and it will make my case."

"What is it?" Judge Grey asked.

"Will you allow me to enter it into evidence?"

"I might," Judge Grey replied.

"And I might move for a mistrial," Legal responded. "Tie up the court system for months with a new trial."

Judge Grey snarled, "Very well, I will allow it. It better be really good. Now I will ask just one more time, what is it?"

"Video footage of one of the abductions of my client," Legal replied.

The gallery erupted into chatter. The Judge slammed his gavel down. "Order!"

Whateley jumped to his feet. "No, I object. You can't just submit more evidence like this."

"We just let you submit yours," Legal replied. "Fair is fair."

Judge Grey hung his head in the realization that he had been played. "Unfortunately, Mr. Legal is correct. I will allow it."

"No," Whateley warned. "It's not safe. You mustn't watch it."

"Normally, it would not be fit for human viewing, but a special friend of mine was able to add safety filters to the clip. It has been authenticated by several reputable sources. It is legit, and it is safe. I have to warn the jury that it is a little racy in parts. However, it will prove my client's case."

"Bailiff, please play the video for the court," Judge Grey said.

"You have all been warned." Whateley shook his finger at the courtroom. "Watch at your own peril."

"Wow, Your Honor." Gary Legal laughed. "You complain about my theatrics. This guy is making a little triple-X action sound like a death sentence."

"Enough. Bailiff, please proceed," Judge Grey decreed. "I will allow no further interruptions to these…"

"No, wait!" Several female members of The Following stepped forward. A sullen woman spoke, "The Following has reconsidered and would like to settle out of court."

"Really?" Legal grinned.

"Yes, we are willing to negotiate. There is no need to play the video."

"Excellent," Gary Legal replied. "All you have to do is cease and desist any contact with Mr. Yrgohlon."

"We understand," the woman replied.

"If you even knock on Mr. Yrgohlon's door to sell him Little Follower cookies, he will sue you hard, and there will be no settling," Gary said. "Do you understand?"

"Yes, we understand," the woman answered.

"Great, I have the papers here. Just step out into the hall with me, and we should be able to get this done in time to beat the rush hour traffic home."

"Does this mean you are getting out of my courtroom?" Judge Grey asked.

"Yes indeed, Your Honor!" Legal replied.

"Good," Judge Grey said. "Don't come back for at least a couple of weeks. Recess for fifteen minutes. I need more Advil."

"Mr. Legal." A small, robe-clad man waved frantically in Gary's direction. "Please, a moment of your time."

Gary could see no other option, given that the man stood with a group directly in the path between Gary and the exit. He stepped forward and held out his hand. "I'm in the middle of a case. How may I help you, sir?"

The man took Legal's hand and shook it vigorously. "We have a case we would like you to consider. The man gazed upon Gary meekly with eyes that had seen much wear and little nourishment.

"Just pop by my office on Monday and talk to Denise. She'll get you started."

"No, Mr. Legal." Another man stepped forward. He was much older and more weathered. "This is a discreet matter. It must remain quiet."

"Okay," Gary replied. "Could you tell me about it after I finish this case?"

"Please." The older man, while the others looked around, seemingly to make sure there were no onlookers. "Our Divine Savior Litroni would like to retain your services."

"I don't know, guys," Gary replied. "I just got through one of these, and it wasn't pretty."

"Our Divine Savior Litroni would be willing to compensate you handsomely."

"It's not about the money, sir. I don't need the money. It's about the principle, and I've had a lot of trouble with you culty types."

"We can telepathically communicate with Litroni," said the smallest of the group. "And…"

"Wait," Gary interrupted. "An hour in the hall outside of this court, okay?"

They all nodded in unison.

Gary left the courtroom before they could say anything else.

"I should have stuck with robots."

Part 5
Gary Legal and the
Outstanding Invoice of Yrgohlon

"Well, that's that," Gary Legal said as he exited the courthouse and jumped into his transport. "Denise!" Legal shouted into his comm unit.

"You don't have to yell," Denise replied.

"Sorry," Gary replied. "Still wound up from the case. Can't wait to divide the spoils. You guys busted your humps for this one. You deserve a good chunk of payola. Those zeros must look nice."

"There are no zeros," Denise replied, deadpan.

"What do you mean, 'no zeroes?'" Gary asked. "Payment was due upon services rendered. Mr. Yrgohlon understood this when he retained my services."

"Well," Denise replied. "There's been no transfer yet."

"Crap," Gary slapped his steering wheel. "Get him on the line."

"One moment." The line went silent, and Gary waited. Denise returned to the call. "He's not answering."

"What?" Gary shook his head. "Keep trying him. Call me back when you get him."

"Yes, Mr. Legal."

Gary ended the call, swung by the donut shop, and headed for the office. The trip back to the office took four donuts and his entire cup of coffee.

"Denise," Gary called out as he entered. "Please give me good news."

"Sorry, Mr. Legal," she replied. "He keeps hanging up on me, and when he did speak, he said you can come get it if you want it."

"Well, doesn't this just suck?" Gary shook his head. "Don't worry. You will all still get bonuses for your hard work. I will personally cover them if this schmuck doesn't pay up."

"I'll be happy if you just don't make me call him again," Denise stated. "He's creepy, even with the filters."

"Check," Gary responded. "No more calling the creepy guy."

Gary sat down in his corner cubicle and pondered his options.

"Mr. Legal," Denise yelled from the front desk.

Gary picked up his comm and called her. "Denise, I did not install this state-of-the-art comm system for us to shout across the office."

"Sorry," Denise replied. "Boy is here to see you."

"Oh? Send him in."

"Re, re," Boy greeted Gary.

"Howdy, what brings you here?"

"Is there something you need help with?" Boy asked. "I need to earn some coin."

"I offered you coin earlier," Gary replied. "You only wanted lunch."

"I want to earn coin, not receive charity."

"Okay, take a seat, please." Gary motioned to the chairs on the opposite side of the desk.

Boy sat in the closest seat.

"I have a problem here," Gary stated. "Maybe you have a perspective on it."

"Me?" Boy asked. "Why me?"

"Because you are not packed into the same neat little box as I am. You can give me a different perspective."

"Because I'm young? Because I hang out in the street? Or because my uncle is a robot?"

"Yes," Gary answered.

"Bindaas!" Boy replied. "What do you need?"

"I have," Gary stated, "a deadbeat client."

"Wait," Boy replied. "Aren't most of your clients deadbeats?"

"No," Gary replied. "Most of my clients are poor but still pay the agreed-upon fees. And if for some reason they can't, they don't just skip out. I have never had a client skip out without paying. And this guy has money."

"Aren't you a lawyer? Can't you do lawyer stuff?"

"Technically, this guy is outside of our jurisdiction."

"What?" Boy asked. "Is he on some other planet?"

"Yes," Gary replied.

"Like the Outer Colonies?"

"A little farther away than that."

"Oh," Boy replied. "If you can't sue him, you don't have much. Unless you go there and take it from him. How much does he owe you?"

"A cool million," Gary replied. "He can afford it. Normally, I wouldn't care, but he is so smug. He said we can come get it if we want it."

"You can't let that slide," Boy replied. "Your cred is on the line."

"My thoughts exactly. Well, it looks like I'm taking a trip. Wanna come along?"

"Seriously?" Boy asked. "Go off world and ditch this city? Faadu!"

"Yeah, for a little while. One more thing. If you come, try to keep the slang to a minimum. I barely understand a thing you say, and we'll need to communicate with each other. Can you stick to English?"

"Achha!" Boy grinned. "Of course."

The spaceport was bustling with vacationers and business travelers. Each patron focused on his or her own personal travel dramas. For some, this would be their first time off world; for others, it was routine. No matter what the situation, it was never easy. The spacelines pulled out every trick from their arsenal to gouge passengers and maximize profits. That's why Gary Legal never flew commercial. Besides, nobody offered flights to where he intended to go.

Gary Legal deactivated his comm in sheer frustration.

"Still not answering?" Boy asked.

Gary shook his head. "This guy is playing it hard."

"So, we're going?"

"Looks that way," Gary responded.

"Faadu!"

"Okay, Boy," Gary started. "Follow my lead. Don't let anything I say offend you. Hold any questions until I tell you it's time. Got it?"

Boy nodded. "Achha."

Gary shook his head. "I'll take it that means 'yes.' Come on."

Gary expertly navigated the spaceport, delivering the pair in front of a dingy counter in the economy wing of the facility.

"They ask fewer questions here," Gary advised Boy. "Watch and learn."

Gary turned his attention to the man behind the counter. He was a forty-something with a twenty-something surfer haircut. His tanned, weathered skin clashed with his greasy blond hair. He leaned back in his chair, his feet up on the counter, gazing out bleary-eyed at the sea of competing low-budget concession stands.

"Good morning, Dave." Gary offered his hand.

Dave dragged himself upright and eagerly shook Gary's hand. "Good to see you, my friend."

218

"Midsized eco job. Six to eight-week trip." Gary said. "Standard deal?"

"Who's taking 'er out?" Dave asked.

"Me and Boy here," Gary answered.

Dave raised an eyebrow. "Destination?"

"Outer Colonies…ish."

"Ish?"

"Ish."

Dave nodded. "Okay, but that's going to cost a little more."

"Okay," Gary agreed. "But no logs, no receipts."

"Six coins," Dave replied.

"Are you insane?" Gary asked. "Six coins for a masterpiece from your spectacular fleet? That's a whole coin a week, and I didn't see anything that could be mistaken for a luxury brand out there."

"Ish," Dave pointed out.

Gary sneered. "Two coins. Be reasonable."

"I wouldn't rent a ship to my mother for two coins for six to eight weeks going to ish."

"Three coins, and I agree to pay any damage."

"Damage fees are already part of the standard agreement."

"But I always pay," Gary pointed out.

"You do," Dave nodded. "Okay, four coins."

"Three point five."

Dave held out his hand. "Deal."

Gary took his hand and shook vigorously. "Boy, pay the man."

"Huh?" Boy appeared bemused.

"Just kidding," Gary reached into his coat pocket, pulled out three and a half cash coins, and dropped them on the table.

Dave handed him some keys.

"It's in one piece?" Gary asked.

"Yup," Dave replied.

"It runs."

"It runs great."

"Okay. We good with the deal?"

"We're good," Dave answered. "Teal Omni in the third row."

"A Suzuki Maruti?" Gary rolled his eyes. "Of course it is."

The Omni was not pretty. It was just about as plain and economy class as it got, but it was in one piece and appeared to be in working order. Gary Legal and Boy boarded, throwing their bags in the lone sleeping compartment.

"Welcome to the marriage crusher," Gary announced. "A ship too sexy to compete with your wife."

"It's…whole."

Gary chuckled. "That's an excellent way of putting it. And look, it has abundant accommodations for one."

"Koi Na," Boy said. "I'll sleep on the floor."

"Nobody is sleeping on the floor. We sleep in shifts. I don't trust the autopilot on this technological marvel."

"Okay," Boy replied. "So, where does this guy live?"

"Basically, past the Outer Colonies and hook a left for about a week." Gary started entering the coordinates into the navigation system. The console chirped a response in a cheerful but slightly warbled tone.

"It's over three weeks just to get to the Outer Colonies. You told Dave six weeks."

"Yeah, he didn't need to know that. He would have hiked up the price upfront. Late charges are easy to haggle. Strap in for launch."

"You lied to him?" Boy buckled himself into his seat.

"Nah, I erred on the side of optimism. Maybe we'll make good time. Besides, you can't foresee every delay in a trip. He'll understand. He always does." Gary got the clearance to launch and took off. In moments, the ship had escaped the Earth's atmosphere and began its course out toward the Outer Colonies.

"This guy must have a lot of coin to live alone out there. I hear some crazy tatti floating around. What is he? Some kind of paynet vid-stream kiddie?"

"Well, no." Gary Legal massaged his neck and stretched it from side to side. "He's more of a celebrity. You know, a character."

"He has to make coin somehow. Is he a comic or something?"

"He's something. Kind of a religious figure."

"So, he's a paynet prophet?"

"Eh," Gary replied. "Think bigger, much bigger."

"What do you mean? I don't understand."

"He's an…er…elder god," Gary muttered.

"A what, what? Did you just say 'God'?"

"Yes," Gary responded. "Yes, I did say 'god'."

"We're collecting from an old guy who thinks he's a god?"

"No, we are collecting from Yrgohlon the Unfathomable, who hired me to do a cease and desist on a bunch of kooky cultists. I won; he didn't pay."

"You said 'God,'' Boy muttered.

"We already covered that, buddy."

"How are we going to make him pay?" Boy asked. "You can't make God pay. What if he smites us or something?"

"He's not God, he's a god, with a small 'g.' Besides, you were all keen on the trip before we left."

"That was before you told me he was a god. I'm going to die."

"Nobody's going to die," Gary responded. "We're just going to pop over there and enforce our terms. He can afford it."

"What kind of powers does this guy have?"

"Powers?"

"You said he's a god. Gods have powers."

"I don't know," Gary shrugged. "He's got this insanity, chaos thing going."

"Insanity?" Boy whined. "How does that work?"

"I dunno," Gary answered. "If you look at him, you go batshit crazy. You should have seen the cultists. They went bonkers just by reading about the guy."

Boy shook his head. "How did you even meet with him? Unless you already went insane." Boy tried to jump out of his chair, forgetting he was strapped in.

"Settle down. I'm not insane. First, I met with an intermediary in the Dream Realm. That was weird. There were lots of cats. Moon cats. Who would have thought?"

Boy stared at Gary like he had grown a second head.

"Relax. I met with the guy via filtered netchat. Your uncle set up the algorithm to protect my fragile human psyche. I'm fine."

Boy continued to glare at Gary.

"You saw the video he processed. You were okay, remember?"

"Wait, that horror movie for your court case with the sex and human sacrifices was *real*? We're gonna go see that thing?"

"Hey, he didn't ask for any of that. Those cultists decided to do all that sex and sacrifice stuff all on their own. Hence the cease and desist."

"Why didn't he pay?"

"Maybe he's one of those guys who stays rich by not paying his bills. But he said to come get it. Well, I'm coming to get it."

"I'm going to die," Boy lamented.

"Buck up." Gary grinned. "Enjoy the road trip. Wanna stop by Kang's on the way?"

"Kang's? What's that?"

"Out of the Bubble. You never stopped there?"

"What is it?"

"Only the best tourist trap anywhere. It's just outside of the solar system. We are so stopping. Wait until you see Helmets Around the Galaxy."

"Okay." Boy still looked fairly shaken.

"You look tired. Why don't you take the bunk for now and get some shut-eye?"

"Okay." Boy unlatched his safety harness and dragged himself back to the sleeping compartment. It was not long before he passed out, and an even shorter time until he started snoring.

Gary turned on some music and hummed along with the tunes. It helped drown out the snoring and aided in keeping Gary alert.

After a few hours, Boy stirred. He plodded over to the chair next to Gary's and sunk into it. He rubbed his bleary eyes with his shirt sleeve.

"Feeling any better?" Gary asked.

"Tea."

"I got it." Gary got up and grabbed two cups of Insto-T. He pulled the bottom tab, and the tea heated to a perfect sipping temperature. He handed a cup to Boy.

Boy eagerly flipped open the lid and inhaled the vapor. He took a sip and choked.

"I didn't say good tea," Gary pointed out.

Boy took another sip. "It'll work. I'm glad to have it."

"That's awfully Zen of you," Gary said.

Boy shrugged. "G-pop was big into mindfulness. It makes sense to me."

"You're kind of a mish-mosh, aren't you?"

"The world is a mish-mosh."

"True." Gary took a sip of his tea. "This is bad."

"It's hot and caffeinated."

"So is my...never mind. You're right. It's better than nothing."

"Yup. So how do I steer?"

"You don't," Gary explained. "The ship drives itself. But you need to keep an eye on this gauge. About every hour, compare our location to the charts. These old Marutis tend to drift off course."

"What will I do if it drifts?"

"Get me," Gary answered. "Don't let us drift for too long."

"Got it."

Gary took the next shift, and Boy monitored navigation. The pair continued in four-hour shifts. They broke the monotony with meals and old entertainment glimmer drives. Before too long, they were past the protection of the heliosphere and into the vastness of the cosmos.

Soon the Quantum Radio was alive with solicitations.

They advertised everything from engine repair to amusement parks.

"Food, it's what you eat! Come to Kang's Out of the Bubble, where food is guaranteed digestible."

"Digestible," Boy muttered. "What kind of tapri is this?"

"It's fun. Helmets Around the Galaxy."

Boy stared deadpan at the console. "We're drifting again."

"Yeah, seems to do it about every two hours." Gary manually adjusted course. The console chirped its warbled tune at him again.

"Why didn't we just rent one from a big company? One that runs right."

"Because they track you and can shut you down remotely. The last thing I want is to be tractored back to some Podunk rental office somewhere, explaining why I went off-course. Dave is okay with ish."

"But he deals in tatti."

"Unmonitored tatti," Gary stated. "Worth the inconvenience."

"If you say." Boy shrugged. "Hungry. Want some ramen?"

"Nah, we're almost at the home of digestible food. Hang tight."

Minutes later, a flashing sign overtook the expanse before them: Kang's Out of the Bubble. It depicted a caveman foraging for snacks in an ancient refrigeration appliance. Gary pulled into the day parking area.

The attraction was huge. It had a large camping area, two motels, twenty restaurants serving human-style cuisine, and shops as far as the eye could see.

"Meteor boxes?" Boy asked. "Aren't those illegal everywhere but Japan?"

"Not at Kang's," Gary answered. "You should grab a couple. We can launch them as we enter the Earth's atmosphere."

"Didn't one almost take out Fiji?"

"Eh, that was greatly exaggerated, and the meteor box in question was old homemade tech. I knew the attorney on the case. Nobody was even hurt. It's only illegal now because of stupid copyright laws."

"You're not a lawyer," Boy said. "You're like the opposite of that."

"Everyone's a critic."

"You never try to follow the law. Everything's a trick, a technicality. What kind of lawyer does that make you?"

"A good one," Gary replied. "What's your angle? What do you expect?"

"I thought you were a good guy," Boy complained. "You did all that stuff to save my uncle. But you're just shady."

"Sometimes it takes creative law-bending to do the right thing, my friend. It's all about helping people; do no harm."

"Isn't that for doctors?"

"It should be for everyone," Gary responded. "And I'm not shady. I'm a creative thinker. Things aren't always so black and white."

The pair stepped out into the parking lot. A two-meter-tall pylon indicated they were in row Q, section twenty-seven. Gary took note of the location on his comm.

Soon, a man pulled up in a cart, offering them a lift into the facilities. The cart traveled around the perimeter and down the aisles of the parking lot, picking up fellow travelers. A woman sat next to Gary, clutching a fussy baby. The baby whimpered and complained as the woman tried to read a map of her tab. A large gentleman sat next to Boy, forcing him into an awkward angle, half hanging outside off the seat.

"I'm on my way to Earth from the Outer Colonies," the man said to Boy. "It's been a long time since I've been. I'm half afraid it's not still there. Weird, I know."

"It's still there," Boy answered. "Same tatti hole as always."

"Tatti hole?" the man asked.

"Beautiful destination," Gary interjected. "Boy, what did I tell you about that slang?"

Boy frowned.

"Oh, that's okay," the man said. "I can't understand my kids half the time either. Where are you kids off to?"

"It's a working vacation," Gary replied.

"Yeah," Boy added. "We're on our way to collect on an invoice from this deadbeat Yrgohlon."

"Yrgohlon the Unfathomable?" The man reeled back. "I knew a guy who knew this other guy who accidentally drifted into his space. His Maruti stalled out, and he couldn't control his vector. He sent out a distress call. Yrgohlon answered, alright. He tractored in the ship, tortured his mind, and then ripped out his beating heart. People say it hangs on Yrgohlon's rec room wall."

"That is just the most ridiculous story I ever heard. Until the billing snafu, he was perfectly reasonable."

"Well, if I were you, I'd turn around and go home. Forget that invoice. No amount of coin is worth your life and sanity."

"It's a million coins," Gary said.

"Well, better you than me." The man jumped out the second the cart stopped.

Boy scowled at Gary.

"Oh, stop with the look. These are just superstitious hicks. They'll believe anything."

More passengers jumped on the cart, creatively cramming themselves into the finite space. The cart stopped in front of the Earther Shoppe East. Over half of the cart emptied out.

"What do they sell in the Earther Shoppe?" Boy asked, leaning back into his now open seat.

"You know, kitsch," Gary answered. "Earth-style knick-knacks made in the Outer Colonies. Don't worry, we'll check it out."

The next stop was the galaxy's highest space needle, resulting in another large migration of people.

"How high is that?"

Gary shrugged. "Not all that high. They don't specify which galaxy."

Boy nodded. "Clever."

"They're clever, yet I'm shady."

The cart swung around a bend and stopped at the North American Snack Shack.

232

"This is us." Gary tapped Boy's knee as he stood up. "Let's get our digestible food."

The menu was limited to junk food. Gary ordered grease-fried potatoes, a hamdog, and a cola beer. Boy ordered three servings of onion sticks and lemon water. They sat at one of the faux wood tables and consumed their feast.

"They're right," Boy stated. "It is digestible."

"Yeah, it's not bad. Not great, but not bad."

After finishing their meals, the two strolled around the establishment. They purchased some small trinkets from the Human Gear shop. Boy picked up a "genuine old-fashioned multi-tool" complete with a laser cutter, wire clippers, and driver set. Gary picked up a lighter that could ignite in low-air environments. A warning label in red letters stated, "Do not use in high-oxygen environments." It was effectively useless, but it was cool. He also picked up a hat that read Shop Naked at Kang's.

Kang's was massive. However, many of the restaurants and shops were duplicates. One needed to visit only a fraction of the facility to experience all it had to offer. Around the exterior were the motels, the camp area, and the parking lots.

In the center of the premises, the main attraction rose, its glowing beacon glowing overhead for all to see from any spot on the property.

"Wanna check out the space needle?" Gary asked.

"Sure," Boy replied.

"Let's do it!" Gary giggled like a child.

They made their way through the dysfunctional streets of perverted capitalism, passing all manner of travelers. This place was a mecca for the wayward, the weary, and the whiny. Boy's gaze darted wildly, taking in as much as he could consume.

The space needle was still impressive up close despite its faded paint and worn appearance. Boy stepped up and touched the facade of the mammoth structure as if testing its viability.

"You think it's safe?" he asked.

"Sure," Gary replied. "Why wouldn't it be? Come on, let's go."

They stepped into the dimly lit elevator and pushed the up button. The elevator jerked into motion, throwing Boy off balance. Gary caught him by the arm before he fell

234

and sat him on the built-in bench. The speed gradually increased until it felt like a car in a vertical bullet train.

Thirty minutes later, the elevator slowly came to a stop. The doors opened to a glass bubble. The aluminum floor was sticky with spilled drinks and chewing gum. The glass was dirty and smeared with fingerprints and unidentifiable splatters. There was a distinct odor of stale snack food in the air.

The view of the solar system was breathtaking. Fortunately, the dome was angled at a vector, which put the majority of the view directly above it. The glass was relatively clean up top, so all Boy and Gary needed to do was tilt their heads back to behold the beauty of their home system.

"Wow," Boy muttered.

"Yeah," Gary said. "It never gets old."

The two gazed in wonder for several minutes until their moment of peaceful contemplation was shattered.

A small ship darted past the dome, shaking the structure. It whipped around to a stop with its nose pointed toward the main control building of the attraction.

"Did that guy miss the parking signs?" Boy asked.

"Not sure. They are kind of hard to miss. What a douche."

Another small ship swung around, taking a similar position to the first on the other side of Kang's.

"Are those things armed?"

Gary didn't answer immediately. A third ship took its position. Then another and yet another. Soon, eight ships pointed menacing weapons at the tourist trap.

"Yeah, time to go," Gary pushed the button for the elevator, but the readout indicated it was on its way down to the bottom of the shaft. It would be at least forty-five minutes before they could get back down.

"Not good," he stated.

Boy started hunting for emergency override buttons or something to call for help. He found the emergency comm, but it was broken.

"What else can we try?" he asked.

"First, stay calm. Let's ascertain what the situation is before we panic. We don't even know who these guys are. Let me see if I can find a way to listen in on communications."

Gary took out his comm in order to manually hunt for broadcasting comm signals. Normally, they were highly

236

encrypted, but Gary's comm was modified to bypass most encryption algorithms. On Earth, it was a high-priced and extremely illegal hack. Outside of the bubble, it was less expensive and legally ambiguous.

Gary sat on one of the less-soiled benches and began scanning the frequencies.

"…Grandma's tennis balls…"

"Nope." Gary tried another stream.

"…fluid all over. It stinks like…"

"Don't want to know." Gary continued to adjust the signal.

"…pop, pop, pop, pop. Yup, yup…"

"Ho-kay." Gary looked at Boy, who appeared nonplussed about any of the day's events.

"…pay us what you owe, or you will be forcibly removed…"

"We have a winner." Gary locked onto the signal and cranked up the volume.

"We owe you nothing," a different voice responded on the same frequency. "You have been paid in full for a term of two hundred years. There are still seventy-five years left on our lease."

"You will pay the surcharges; the landlord needs a new cruiser." A warning shot grazed the dome, causing Boy to jump backward. A compartment by the elevator opened, revealing one-size-fits-most EVA gear. Boy scrambled to grab two sets.

"We will never cave to extortion." A return shot was fired from a turret projecting out of one of the parking lot pylons.

"Good use of space," Gary commented as he suited up in the EVA suit. Boy had already donned his and was in the process of adjusting his air levels.

"Don't worry," Gary stated. "This thing is made to withstand significant impact."

The dome's loudspeaker crackled to life. "Please enjoy our complimentary fireworks show. Visitors are asked to be patient and remain off our rides while our staff meets for our brief weekly powwow."

Another shot grazed the dome. This time, cracks rapidly spread over the glass.

"Maybe not." Gary tucked his comm into his pocket and sealed himself in. He activated the suit's comm. "Okay, Boy, we're going to have to climb down the side of the ladder."

"It's one hundred thousand meters," Boy whined. "We won't make it."

"We have no choice, buddy. Besides, no gravity, minimum effort."

"I don't…" Before Boy could complete his sentence, another shot shattered the dome completely. The two leaped over the side and hooked onto the ladder. Gary began the climb down. Boy followed clumsily, pausing every few steps to adjust his footing.

"You okay there, buddy? We need to speed this along before this thing gets out of control." Another volley of fire shook the structure.

"Gets out of control?" Boy asked. "Really? What is this?"

"A lovely, complimentary fireworks show," Gary replied. "Keep climbing."

The pair climbed for about half an hour. The explosions continued to shake the tourist trap to the clueless oohs and aahs of the patrons below. Suddenly, Boy stopped.

"Wait," he said.

"Why?" Gary asked.

"Give me the Maruti remote."

"It's in my pocket," Gary said. "I can't get to it, or I'll suffocate."

"Can you feel it through the suit?" Boy asked.

Gary tried. The suit itself was thin. It was made for a single use, so durability was not a factor in its construction. He could just barely feel the remote. "Yeah, I got it."

"Hold on. Get to the side so I can stand next to you."

"It's a little tight for the two of us."

Boy didn't reply. He climbed down next to Gary, each hanging onto the side rail with a death grip. With his free hand, he thumbed his comm. The back was removed from it, and some of the wires were spliced together. Boy held the comm next to Gary's hand that was holding the remote.

"Push the on button," Boy said.

Gary pushed the button. Boy thumbed in some codes into the comm and waited.

"What now?" Gary asked.

"Hold on." Boy's comm blinked and flashed. "Okay."

"Okay, what?"

"Okay, that." Boy pointed behind them to the lighted vehicle quickly approaching.

"Is that the…"

"The Maruti," Boy answered.

"You summoned the Maruti," Gary said with awe. "How did you do that?"

The Maruti pulled alongside the ladder with its emergency airlock lined up with them. They shimmied into the airlock and rushed to the helm. Gary was barely free of his EVA suit when he kicked in the ship's plasma drive.

The ship bucked forward and vibrated very disconcertingly.

"What was that?" Gary asked.

Boy glanced at the ship's status display to check for any issues. "We were hit!"

"Dammit." Gary shook his head. "How bad?"

"Not terrible, but we need to stop soon to fix it, or we'll lose the plasma drive."

"I forgot that you knew all that electronics stuff," Gary said. "Doesn't it pay?"

"Only if you go corp, and the family has that rep, you know."

"Oh, yeah." Gary nodded. "Your G-pop didn't leave that last contract gig on good terms. Thought they would forget about that by now."

Boy shrugged. "Doesn't matter, especially if I diversify."

Gary grinned. "I like that. Diversify."

The ship shuddered again. Boy and Gary exchanged glances.

"There's a planet there." Gary pointed at the navigation readout. "I'll set her down."

Gary was able to land the ship with little trouble. They sat down in a flat field. The grass was low, and aside from a few large boulders, the field appeared empty.

Boy immediately began the repairs. Gary watched in amazement as Boy diagnosed the electrical systems.

"How much longer?" Gary asked.

"A few hours," Boy replied. "I need to get to the plasma circuits, and they're still pretty hot."

"Okay. We should try to be as quick as possible. This place does not show up in any travel logs. I think we're as backwaters as it gets."

"It's better than Kang's." Boy sat on the ground next to the ship and inhaled the fresh air.

242

"Better than Kang's? How can you say such a thing? Where else can you get crap of this caliber? And, I might add, an experience of a lifetime."

"They shot at us."

"They shot at the ship, and we're okay. Plus, you got that cool gadget in the…"

Gary was interrupted by a woman's scream. Boy jumped to his feet.

"No!" Gary stepped forward to block Boy from moving. "Not our problem."

Another scream and Boy pushed Gary aside. He ran full speed to the aid of the unseen victim.

Gary threw his head back and shouted to the sky. "Really?" He ran after Boy. "This is probably a trap. Possibly a legal one. Of massive proportions."

Boy did not stop. He ran until he arrived at an outcropping of trees. There, a half-naked woman on the ground struggled, trying to escape a man standing above her. He had her tied with a rope and was attempting to drag her. The man shouted at the woman. Gary activated the subdermal translator next to his ear.

"…paid for. You are mine."

"Let me go," the woman kicked at the man. "I am not a slave."

"Re! Let her go, phattu," Boy bellowed.

"Look at that, will you?" Gary turned around to see three large men ransacking the ship. "Be back. Don't do anything."

He ran back to the ship, yelling the whole way. He made it to the ship before the group could take too much.

"Drop the goods," Gary demanded.

All three men just laughed. One advanced and challenged Gary. "What are you going to do about it?"

"I'll—" Gary reached into his pocket. All he had was the Maruti remote and the lighter. He pulled out the lighter, grinning when he saw the red lettering, and pointed it at his assailant. "I will ignite you."

They all burst into laughter again. One doubled over, clutching his sides. Gary pointed the lighter a few centimeters to the side of the closest bandit. He leaned back as he clicked to activate it. A six-meter flame erupted past the group. It singed one thug's arm. The field around them smoked and flamed.

Terrified, the men stumbled off, leaving without any of the ship's contents.

244

Soon after, Boy arrived with the woman slung over his shoulder. She kicked and screamed.

"You're safe now," Boy said.

"I think she was with them." Gary pointed at the fleeing men.

Boy put her down and untied her. "Are you alright?" he asked.

"Yes." She scrambled to her feet and wrapped her arms around Boy.

"Thank you," she said. "You saved me. That man kidnapped me."

"What about the dweebs who just tried to rob our ship?" Gary asked.

"I don't know any men that would rob a ship," the woman replied indignantly.

"Of course, you wouldn't," Boy said.

The woman smiled. "Come meet my father so he can reward you. He would certainly want to meet the brave man who saved his favorite daughter."

"Can't," Boy said. "We need to get this chindi chor, Yrgohlon, to pay his bill. But I can come visit another time."

"Yrgohlon the Unfathomable?" the girl gasped. "The last man from my village to face him perished most excruciatingly. His eyes melted, and his skin bubbled."

"Okay, that will be enough of that," Gary interjected.

Boy sneered at Gary. "Mr. Legal assures me that we are perfectly safe."

The woman's eyes grew wide. "You are incredibly brave." She grinned. "Return after your quest. Come to the Yom Village and ask for me. I am Princess Ulka."

She kissed Boy on the cheek and skipped off in the opposite direction of the thugs.

"Of course she is," Gary muttered.

Boy grinned and shook his head. "Don't be hating."

"Fix the ship so we can get out of here already."

Boy nodded and got to work. Gary took the time to load the comm filters in preparation for his conversation with Yrgohlon. They were ready to launch in less than an hour.

Boy took the first sleep shift, being that he had exerted the most energy. Gary relaxed at the controls, keeping an eye on the course. Six hours later, they made the switch. Gary rested, and Boy manned the controls. It went on like that for days. Tedium set in.

246

Boy sighed and slumped over the controls. "Kang's was better than this."

"Stop yer whining…"

The ship's comm burst to life with a loud, piercing sound. Boy screamed, clutching his head. Gary followed.

"It's clawing my brain," Boy screamed.

"Hang on," Gary dug his fingers into his chair. "The mind scraping will stop in a second."

"I can't take it." Boy collapsed to the floor and started to whimper.

"I know…it's difficult," Gary said. "It will pass."

"I think I'm hallucinating…"

"You are, buddy, you are…"

The sound died out, and the ship stopped in what looked like a cavern in space. The area was warped and twisted. Impossible angles bent and folded around the Maruti. Gary peered out of the viewport, then shook his head as if he was trying to dislodge the insanity.

"Well, I've never seen space throb like that," he stated.

Boy stood up and gazed out the window. "What is that?"

"The celestial lair of Yrgohlon the Unfathomable," Gary answered.

"No, sir, I don't like it."

The comm sounded again. This time with a deep but grating voice. "Who dares trespass on the domain of Yrgohlon?"

"Um," Gary replied. "Gary Legal. I'm here about the outstanding invoice."

"Yrgohlon the Unfathomable does not deal with invoices!"

"I would disagree with that, buddy. He agreed to payment in full when he signed the contract to retain my services."

"Yeah!" Boy added.

"Yrgohlon does not retain services. Yrgohlon is—" The comm went silent for a moment, and the sounds of muffled voices sounded through the speaker.

"Wait. We were just informed that Yrgohlon did indeed retain the services of Gary Legal. We will provide you payment immediately. Please allow us access to your cargo area so we may pay you in precious metals."

"Sure, but I don't understand. Why didn't you just transfer the funds to my account like we agreed upon?"

248

"Oh, since they upgraded us to quantum beam, our data connection has been spotty at best. Can't even get Galizon to come out and fix it. Our comms don't work right. All our calls dropped. That's why Yrgohlon said to come get it. He couldn't even stay connected to your assistant long enough to explain. Sorry about that."

"Yeah, but what about all those people you tortured and killed?" Boy demanded. "I heard the stories."

"Mostly just stories. We let the rumors flow. This keeps the solicitors away."

"Mostly," Boy muttered. "No wonder Galizon won't show."

"Well, that's that," Gary stated. "Thank you for your patronage. Please tell Yrgohlon that it was a pleasure doing business with him. Any time he needs legal services, keep us in mind."

"What?" Boy asked indignantly. "After all that tatti, you want to do business with this guy again?"

"Hey," Gary shrugged. "In this business, the customer is always right."

Part 6
Gary Legal and the Martin Law Firm

"That's the thing, Your Honor!" Gary exclaimed. "You can't stop them. Why would you want to stop them? We all know that Japanese robots love to dance. Look at that happy little bugger. How can you reprogram him and erase all the joy off his perky little face?"

"Mr. Legal," the judge bellowed, "save your theatrics for the courtroom. All I'm asking is if there is any way we can avoid a trial. The courts are flooded with Outer Colony permit applications. I want to be with my family on Christmas. How can I get you two to settle this quickly?"

"You can't." Paulie Martin yawned and gazed at his watch. "Legal is going to make this into one of his crazy dramas. Listen, I gotta go. I have a ten o'clock."

"You go when I tell you to go," the judge replied. "Just answer the question."

Paulie shook his head. "This is a domestic robot, not a dancebot. It was purchased to clean the freakin' house, not strut around to pop music. It is within the owner's rights to wipe and reload it."

Gary pulled out his tab and played a clip of the robot dancing. "Look how happy he is. How can you be so mean?"

"It's a robot, a device. It was purchased from a store. Meanness is irrelevant."

"Well, then you wouldn't mind if Mr. GoCleanBot pays off his term of service with your client."

"There is no way that is going to happen," Paulie stated. "We are not settling. This law firm stands strongly by its convictions. We will not placate these gear-hugger freaks who insist on anthropomorphizing toasters. These are machines. They don't have rights. They are consumer products designed to function as tools. So no, we will not help you set some kind of precedent."

"If you settle, we won't be setting any precedents," Gary replied. "But, if we go to trial and I win, we will."

"Win? You can't win." Paulie scoffed. "We will fight this until you run out of resources and give up."

"So that's how we're going to play this?" Gary asked. "You want to play this hard, no compromises."

"Did I stutter?" Paulie responded. "We will not settle."

"Sorry, Your Honor," Gary apologized. "I tried."

"Save it, Legal," the judge replied. "Somehow, all your cases end up being a pain in the ass. The trial is set to begin on the 23rd. I would appreciate a quick trial without too many surprises. Now get the hell out of my chambers, both of you."

Gary didn't even look at Paulie Martin. He simply tucked his tab back into his pocket and stepped out of the office.

"Here we go," he muttered as he pulled out his comm.

"Re, re…" Boy answered from the other end of the call.

"Hey, Boy," Gary greeted.

"How'd it go?" Boy asked.

"As expected," Gary answered.

"That bad. So, what's the plan?"

"The plan is the plan. Contact your uncle. Tell him it's on."

"Consider it done."

"We shall speak of this no more."

"Roger that," Boy replied.

Paulie left the judge's chambers and proceeded to the court clerk's office.

"Hey, Amber." Paulie smiled at the clerk behind the counter. "You should have some files waiting for me."

"Let me check that for you, sweetie," Amber cooed.

"Thank you, beautiful." Paulie winked.

Amber smirked as she entered the appropriate keystrokes. The workstation responded with the sound of a discordant trombone. Amber pushed the keys again and once more. An expression of frustration crossed her face.

"I'm sorry, Mr. Martin." She tapped the back of her screen. "It's not responding."

"Well, try again," Paulie replied.

"I'm trying again, Mr. Martin. It won't load. I'll call the IT bot and get it fixed."

"I'll be back," Paulie stated. "I'll check in after my next case."

"I'll be here, sweetie." Amber forced a smile.

Paulie crossed the ground to the old courthouse, Building One. It was an old brick building, a throwback to the pre-tech era. Although it had been modernized with all the latest technologies, it still had an inescapable retro feel. Paulie found it profoundly comforting.

Paulie stepped into the lobby and locked his comm and lappad in one of the lockers. He had met with his client the previous afternoon, so they planned to meet outside the courtroom right before court was in session.

"Mr. Smith," Paulie greeted his client. "Good to see you. Ready to go?"

Mr. Smith was an elderly man who walked with a cane. His face twisted into a cross between a smile and a sneer. "You betcha! I'm ready to stick it to those bastards. My lawn still looks like a mud pit. Damned robots have no sense of urgency."

"We're showing them the value of proper lawn care," Paulie replied.

The pair entered the courtroom and found seats towards the front. Just as Paulie took his seat, the power went out. People started complaining and moving around the room.

"Everyone settle down," the bailiff said. "The power should be back on in a moment."

Paulie and Mr. Smith remained seated. Mr. Smith, however, grew impatient when the environmental controls continued to remain off.

"It's hot in here," he complained. "Can we open a window?"

Paulie didn't answer. He simply watched the others fidgeting and fussing. The temperature was indeed creeping up, and the mood was unpleasant.

"Okay, people, it looks like there is a glitch in the power systems. The power backups should have kicked in by now. So we're going to take an hour's recess while maintenance works on the problem. Everyone be back here in an hour."

Paulie didn't relish the idea of spending that time with his client. Now, he would have to spend an hour listening to complaints about the state of modern culture and how much better things were fifty years ago. Maybe if Paulie could keep Mr. Smith's attention on the case, he could avoid the curmudgeon routine.

Paulie grabbed his briefcase and stood up. "Well, Mr. Smith, let's go ride it out in the cafeteria over a cool drink."

Mr. Smith stood up and nodded. "Good idea. I certainly could go for a lemonade. I wonder if they make it the right way here or use that powdered garbage."

"I think they have it in a bottle," Paulie replied.

The pair made their way out of the courtroom and into the lobby. They each reclaimed their electronics from their respective lockers. That's when power returned to the building.

"That was quick," Paulie said.

"That's what happens when you let humans do the work," Mr. Smith replied, "instead of these infernal robots. Can't trust a machine to do a man's job."

Paulie had nothing personal against the machines. They never did him any wrong. But he was a partner in Martin and Martin, the law firm for the people, not the robots. So, his public stance was very clear. And people like Mr. Smith, who comprised most of his clientele, had a certain expectation of Paulie's opinions. "The cafeteria is this way," Paulie stated.

Paulie and Mr. Smith discussed the case over beverages and snacks before returning to the courtroom. Again, they stowed their electronics in the lockers and entered the courthouse.

The courtroom was halfway filled when the two entered. They took their seats and waited. A few more people shuffled in; the room started filling.

Paulie pulled out his notes and began getting into the zone. He focused on the case and the feeling he had each time he won. Feeling centered, Paulie was ready. He grinned.

The power went off.

"Damn it!" someone yelled from the back.

The bailiff pulled out his comm and made a call. Paulie watched him nod and motion with his free hand. After a moment, he frowned and shook his head.

"Okay, we're calling it. All your cases are going to be rescheduled for next week."

Grumbles sounded from the courtroom.

"Enough of this nonsense." Mr. Smith stood up. "I blew off my golf game for this."

He walked out of the courtroom, and Paulie followed. Just as they crossed the threshold, the power came back on.

"This is madness," someone from inside the courtroom bellowed.

"Should we try to get through some cases?" the bailiff asked the judge. "Before we lose power again?"

"Yes," the judge replied. "Let's skip the formalities and jump into it. My first case is…" The judge swiped through his casepad. "Mr. Smith, are you still here?"

Mr. Smith stepped back into the courtroom. "Yes, I'm still here."

"Good. Is your legal counsel still here, too?"

"Here, Your Honor." Paulie stepped into the courtroom behind Mr. Smith.

"Good, let's get this done. Mr. Smith, you're claiming—"

The power went out again.

"That's it," the judge said. "We're done." He stood up and left without allowing the bailiff a chance to have the courtroom rise.

"Well, you heard him," the bailiff said. "Reschedule your cases."

Everyone shuffled out past Paulie and Mr. Smith, groaning and muttering.

"I'll get this rescheduled and call you," Paulie said.

Mr. Smith nodded. "I'll wait to hear from you."

Paulie shook Mr. Smith's hand, and the pair departed.

Paulie headed back to the office—but first, he needed to make one quick stop.

He pulled into the parking lot, relieved that it was not full. It was the middle of the day, so no crowds. Now Paulie only had to haggle for fresh. He needed his fix.

"Hello, Mr. Martin," the man behind the counter greeted him.

"Good afternoon, Cezar," Paulie replied. "What's fresh?"

Cezar frowned. "Nothing. The batterbot went down this morning. I tried to reset it, but it's still offline."

"Crap," Paulie complained. "My day keeps getting better."

"If you can wait, I have some batter in the refrigerator. I can fry up a fresh batch for you. It will take about fifteen minutes."

"Yes, thank you." Paulie nodded. "I'll take some coffee while I wait."

"You got it." Cezar prepared a black coffee for Paulie.

Paulie took a sip. "Mmm, you make the best coffee."

"Thank you," Cezar replied. "Yell if someone comes in."

Cezar went to the back to prepare Paulie's fix.

Paulie sipped his coffee and stared out the shop window, wondering what would go wrong next. He checked his comm for any messages. He didn't see anything new.

A loud thud and crash sounded from the kitchen in the back.

"What the freakin' hell?" Paulie complained.

"Fryer's out," Cezar announced as he stepped out behind the counter. "The logic circuits crashed. Can't make anything now."

"Perfect." Paulie sighed. He reached into his pocket and handed Cezar enough cashcoins to cover the coffee.

"Sorry," Cezar said. "Come back tomorrow. I'll make you something good."

"Thanks," Paulie replied. "Appreciate it."

Paulie stepped out of the shop and returned to his transport.

He turned on some music and flipped through the stations, looking for something calming. He swiped until he found some easy listening. Soothing tunes filled the cabin, flushing away the troubles of the day. Violins and piano melodies coaxed Paulie's blood pressure down. He let out a sigh of relief as he started the drive back to the office.

He merged into the superway, feeling somewhat less stressed. He activated his comm to check in with the office. There was no response. He tried again. He got nothing but dead air. He tried a random contact, his dry cleaner. He got nothing.

Then his music started to drift. What had been blissful, comforting music was now caustic, pulse-quickening botpop. Paulie almost lost control of his transport when the feed changed. He tried another station, but the feed remained unchanged. He powered it off. It came back on and increased in volume.

Paulie now had a massive headache.

He arrived at his office and parked in his spot. The botpop continued to blare out from inside of the transport. He clutched his temples and proceeded to go inside.

As Paulie entered, an intern ran into him.

"Sorry, Mr. Martin," he said. "Things are a little crazy here."

Paulie looked around. The office was in complete chaos. The lights flickered; the environmental alarms blared. People were running back and forth in the hallways, all the monitors at the front desk were running test patterns, smoke was coming out of the kitchen, and there was a lot of yelling.

"What's going on?" Paulie asked.

"We don't know," the intern replied. "But the machines stopped working."

"Machines? Which machines?

"All of them, sir."

A crash sounded from beyond the reception area.

"I have to check that, sir."

Paulie nodded. "Yes, go ahead."

The intern ran in the direction of the sound. Paulie continued walking down the hallway in the direction of his brother's office.

He shook his head as he watched the assistants and IT staff dashing from office to office, attempting to quell the pandemonium. He stepped into Donnie's office to find him shouting orders at one of the clerks. She was clearly shaken.

"Hey, Donnie."

"Don't hey me," Donnie replied. "Where have you been? The place is going crazy. I've been calling you all day."

"My comm's down. What happened?"

"What does it look like happened? Every device that runs off electricity is going haywire."

"Your pencil sharpener looks fine."

"Okay, wise-ass. Anything with a computer chip is malfunctioning. Is that precise enough for you?"

"What time did it start?" Paulie asked.

"Somewhere before ten this morning."

"That's what I was afraid of. Tell everyone to keep their comms off. I think they're tracking us through them. Can the staff work from home?"

"Who exactly is tracking us?"

"Legal's robots," Paulie answered. "This started when I refused to settle the Cleanbot case. I think he's trying to strong-arm us."

"That's illegal. We should call the cops."

"And tell them what? We have no proof."

"Maybe you should settle and let him have this one."

"Dad said never to settle robot cases. We have a reputation to never let the robots get away with it."

"Then what?" Donnie asked.

"I'll call Legal and see if I can get him to see reason."

"Good luck with that."

Paulie activated his comm. The display indicated that he had no reception. He was unable to load email or any data. As he searched through his address book, trying to locate Gary Legal's number, the data connection was re-established. A text message appeared from an unknown number.

"Ready to negotiate?" it read.

"We don't negotiate with terrorists," Paulie replied back.

"What's he saying?" Donnie asked.

"Nothing yet," Paulie replied. "Hold on."

A new text appeared. "Not terrorism, passive resistance. Nobody's been hurt, only inconvenienced. It appears your office help is unhappy with your company's policies."

Paulie glanced over at Donnie's tab screen, which had the words "Screw you" bouncing around it at different angles.

"No machine is going to bully me into submission," Paulie entered.

"Okay, your call." The comm flashed and powered off.

"Dad is going to have a shit fit," Donnie stated. "We can't tell him about this."

"Tell him? He'll see it when he walks in."

"I'll have Mom distract him. Just until we figure this out."

"Why?" Paulie asked. "We could use his help."

"Because he'll think we can't run this on our own. I just got him down to two days a week. I don't need the added pressure."

"This has nothing to do with you," Paulie said. "Don't worry, I'll take the heat. Where is he now?"

"He *was* at some charity luncheon with Mom," Donnie replied. "He's on his way."

"Good. Maybe he can snap Legal back in line. I'll be in my office."

"I wouldn't go in there," Donnie said. "The machines are unhappy with you."

"Just me?" Paulie replied.

"Mostly you," Donnie answered.

"Great." Paulie left his brother's office and headed down the hallway. He passed his father's office, which was a plush glass-and-wood tribute to all things law.

Bookshelves lined the walls, framing the Herman Miller mahogany desk. A single light shone down and illuminated the desk like a monument to pretension.

Paulie's office was somewhat less ostentatious. Unlike his father and brother, Paulie was never one for flash. It was comfortable and functional. The desk was glass and aluminum, stylish but understated. The chairs were aluminum and ivory suede. The walls held little other than Paulie's credentials, with only one bookshelf holding a few obligatory law journals and little else.

Paulie was surprised to find that his office was intact. Not a single piece of paper was out of place, the lighting was steady, and all was calm. He entered the room cautiously, fearful that the room might be lying in wait for a trap to spring. He took a deep breath and stepped inside.

Nothing happened.

Paulie took a seat at his desk. He flipped on the news feeds. The regular drivel filled the screens. A dispute continued to rage over the increased Martian luxury tax. The second non-corporate, civilian transport of colonists departed for the new Outer Colonies. And a local man was up in arms over a glitch in his doughnut-making robot. Paulie activated the audio on the clip.

"…a menace," the man stated. "No problems up until today. Suddenly, the thing refuses to work. It just shuts itself off. The last time I tried, it gave me the middle finger."

"Information is still coming in," the reporter added. "Several local businesses have come forward with reports of systematic malfunctions. Like this doughnut shop, restaurants and fuel stations around the area are out of business today, reporting their robots simply will not function. There is no pattern yet. These robots do not share a common manufacturer or type. And not all businesses have been impacted. In fact, there is no geographic pattern for the affected businesses. They are scattered throughout the city."

Another reporter chimed in. "We are now hearing that there were reports of problems in the county judicial center. Can you confirm?"

"Yes," the original reporter replied. "Reports have been confirmed that the courthouse was experiencing similar problems earlier this morning. However, all of those issues have appeared to have passed for now.

Investigators are searching for a link between the incidents. They have not yet ruled out terrorism."

"Terrorism?" Paulie muttered to himself. "Great."

He flipped off the news feed and leaned back in his chair. A moment later, his desk comm buzzed.

"Dad's here," Donnie announced through the speaker.

"Good," Paulie replied. "He'll tell me how to fix this disaster."

Marty Martin was not a man to be trifled with. He was a man of average build, with the appearance of being well-fed. Despite his rounded form, he was feared. In the legal field, he was considered one of the most ferocious. His firm's success was a direct result of his aggression and tenacity.

He lumbered down the hall and into Paulie's office. "Your brother says you know something about this bullshit."

"Yeah," Paulie answered. "I need your help. Maybe you can help me get Legal off my back."

"Legal?" Marty asked. "Gary Legal, that bleeding heart, activist, pain in the law's ass?"

"Yes, that one," Paulie replied. "He's making it hard on the Johnson dancing robot case. He's representing the little bastard."

"When did he move on from defending ghetto trash to being the champion for broken vacuums?"

"He's been at it for a while," Paulie answered. "Rumor has it he was involved in some big hush-hush government case. After that, he started protecting consumer electronics."

"Strange timing," Marty stated. "He must have pissed off someone extremely connected to shift gears this way. No pun intended."

Paulie grimaced. "Can you talk to his father? Maybe he can get him to back off."

"Talk to Mel Siegel about Gary?" Marty shook his head. "Terrible idea. All we'll do is make an enemy of Siegel. He does not discuss his son, and I don't want to piss that guy off. He'll bury us. No, you need to find another angle."

"I'm out of angles. Legal's clients know everywhere I go and are in the process of making me suspect number one."

"What did you do to piss him off?"

"I refused to settle the case," Paulie replied.

"Why?" Marty asked.

"Because you told me that we never settle robot cases. Because we are the law firm of the people, not the robots. Because Legal is so goddamn smug."

Marty sighed and shook his head. "You should know better. When I say 'never,' it never means 'NEVER.' It means never settle unless it benefits the client and us—especially us. I'd expect this black-and-white thinking from your brother, but not you."

"Now you tell me." Paulie shook his head. "It doesn't matter. I can't back down now. I'll look weak to Legal, and that's the last thing we need."

"Well, it's your call. I'm out of this but keep this robot vengeance shit out of the office. It's killing productivity."

"I'll stay out of here until this is done." Paulie sighed. "What would you do, Dad?"

"I would weigh my options and choose the one with the most to gain and the least to lose. Sometimes, we have to deal now to put ourselves in a better position to attack later." Marty stood up and headed out the door.

Paulie nodded. "Maybe Legal will cave if I don't roll over like he expects."

Marty laughed. "Don't underestimate the persistence on that one. He's tenacious."

"Great."

Marty left Paulie alone with his thoughts. Paulie wasn't feeling any better.

He sat, pondering his options. On one hand, he didn't like Legal's tactics. He was sneaky and conniving. On the other hand, he had to admire his persistence. But why persist so tirelessly for the sake of machines? What could possibly drive a man to waste his efforts on something as fleeting as consumer robotics? These things were made to be replaced.

Paulie picked up his comm and replied to Legal's last message. "Why?"

It took a few moments before he got a response.

"Pubster's, twenty minutes."

Paulie was familiar with Pubster's. It was a hole where people went to be lame. Nothing ever happened there, but the drinks were cheap, and it was clean. This made it the perfect neutral ground to engage the enemy.

When Paulie arrived, Gary Legal was already seated at a back table with a pitcher of beer. He waved Paulie over with a smile. Paulie approached apprehensively.

"Here, sit." Gary motioned to the chair across from him. "Have a beer. I know you're having a crappy day."

"Thanks." Paulie sat and poured beer into his waiting glass. He took a sip. It was cold and satisfying.

Neither man spoke for a moment. Each sat and sipped their drink, enjoying the tranquility of the moment.

Gary broke the silence. "You asked why. Why what, specifically?"

Paulie leaned forward over his beer. He clasped it tight like it was his most important possession.

"Why this bullshit?" he asked. "With the robots. I know they can't pay that much."

Gary shrugged. "It's not about the money. Never was."

"I don't understand. I met your father. How is that possible?"

"You mean, how is it possible that any son of my father could forgo the trappings of luxurious living for a life of defending the little guy?"

"Kinda," Paulie replied. "What gives? Why do you care?"

"Why do I care?" Gary sighed and glanced up at the ceiling. "I guess it started with Shanie."

"Shanie? A girl?"

"Yeah," Gary grinned. "She was as cute as a button. She used to remind me of the color orange, the way she glowed. She'd walk into a room, and happiness would follow. It took me months to build up the courage to ask her out. We studied together for the entire first semester. She was so smart, the smartest person I know."

"Did she dump you?" Paulie asked. "Break your heart?"

"No." Gary shook his head. "No, it was all me. I…she was not privileged. She worked every angle so she could get into that school. She got perfect grades and test scores. She participated in every extracurricular activity that would reflect well on her application. She hustled like nobody I've ever met. And she did it with joy. She deserved nothing but good things, and she…uh…ended up with me. Well, for a little while."

"What did you do?"

"Uh," Gary winced. "I let my fear make my decision. My Dad made a surprise visit when I was in class, and my roommate was there. My roommate was a dick and told my father that I was dating classless ghetto trash. My Dad physically pulled me out of my philosophy class. I was so embarrassed. I tried to talk to him and tell him how amazing Shanie was. He wouldn't hear anything. He told me he'd stop paying my tuition if I kept seeing the girl. So, I caved. I was scared. I told Shanie the truth. She kissed me on the cheek and told me that she was sorry for me, trapped in my prison. We never spoke again."

Gary smirked. "But they were the best two weeks of my collegiate experience."

"So that's why you tortured your father over a girl? That's why you do this?"

Gary shook his head. "Nah. Maybe at first. But I got over that."

"Then why? Why these senseless shit attacks? Who cares about a few machines?"

"I do. I care about Al and the tank. I care about poor dead caddibot and that poor little bastard who only wants to dance. Shanie was right. I was in a prison, but I created that prison. These poor schmoes are built into their prisons, and nobody is willing to stand up for them."

"Whoa." Paulie put his hands up as he leaned back in his chair. "Those are all robots? There's a robot named Al?"

"Yeah," Gary answered. "He's a friend of mine. He almost didn't make it."

"You're friends with a robot. What do you even talk about?"

"I dunno, stuff. He's a hell of a poker player."

Paulie glared at Gary. "And you were friends with a dead caddibot?'

"Well," Gary replied. "He wasn't dead when we met, and he was more like a pet than a friend. But he got a really bad deal."

Paulie finished his beer and poured another glass. He gulped down half of it and put it down. "So, this is a calling, a cause. It's not some kind of Mel Siegel golden opportunity. There isn't some lucrative scheme. I won't win."

"Sorry, buddy," Gary said. "I'm not caving."

Paulie nodded. "Okay, asshole, we'll settle. But we keep it quiet. I don't need this reflecting badly on the firm."

"You got it." Gary held out his hand.

Paulie shook Gary's hand and then finished his beer. He stood up. "And no more mechanical theatrics, right?"

"You keep up your end of the bargain, and we'll all be fine."

"Good, because I'm getting a goddamned donut on the way home."

"You go get your donut." Gary grinned and winked at Paulie.

Paulie grunted as he left the pub. He jumped into his car with a single destination in mind. When he arrived, Cezar was waiting with a steaming-hot box of old fashions. The batterbot was chugging along happily in the kitchen.

His comm buzzed. It was his father.

"Hey, Dad."

"Did you resolve your problem?"

"Yeah," Paulie answered. "How did you know?"

"The copier stopped jamming. Are you alright?"

"Yeah, I am now."

"Good," Martin replied. "Bring me back some donuts, too."

"Donuts? What donuts?"

Martin laughed. "See you soon."

276

The call ended, and Paulie pulled out a donut. He took a bite.

Part 7
Gary Legal, Space Attorney

The government building could have been anywhere for any department. Its cinder block walls were painted in pale, muted tones, showing no hint of passion or individuality. It was intentionally generic. A vid streamer hung on the wall, blaring daytime programming for the few people unfortunate enough to be stuck waiting in the lobby. Next to the vid, an office door hung open. One man sat behind a barren desk while two others stood in front of the desk, speaking to the man.

"Results, agents?" the man behind the desk asked.

"I got nothing, Mr. Secretary," one of the agents replied. "I tried every type of honey trap; we tried any configuration we could think of. Sex would not work."

The secretary shook his head. "Do we have anything else?"

"No," said the other agent. "We tried drugs, bribery, blackmail, flattery—and forget physical confrontation."

"Are they that formidable?" asked the secretary.

"Yes," the two agents answered in unison.

The jingle from a cleaning product commercial made its way into the office from the waiting area: "Make it clean, smells so free, the way it ought to be. Smells so free, happy me, buy it now, you'll see!"

"They are several times stronger than us, devote their entire being to the pursuit of logic and positive advancement, and are unaffected by any kind of temptation," the first agent said.

"We have no plan," the second agent added.

"We need to get our hands on their technology," the secretary growled. "You are supposed to be the best agents we have. You have each toppled entire governments single-handedly. You mean to tell me that you can't get your hands on a single piece of tech?"

"We have tried every kind of convincing." The first shook his head. "They are impossible, impossible."

"There is no way," the second agent lamented.

"So, we should just give up?" the secretary asked. "We should just do as they say and develop naturally and remain at a technical disadvantage."

Both agents shrugged.

"Have you got legal problems?" the vid blared. "Circumstantial evidence got you looking guilty, but nobody believes you? I will! Is your boss making you work free overtime? We can make that cheapskate pay!

Have you been refused medical services due to the 'Too Poor to Live' laws? Come to the offices of Gary Legal and let me help you!"

The agents looked at each other and back to the secretary. They all smiled.

"Okay, Boy," Gary said. "Just follow my lead. I've dealt with these pompous types all my life. They are all blah, blah, blah, and full of hot air. But there's no substance. Don't let them intimidate you, no matter what they threaten you with. And take off that music dump already."

"Threaten?" Boy pulled off his earphones. Music blared out of the digital music player's main speaker for a moment before he powered it off. He was visibly uncomfortable. A bead of sweat ran down his face.

"Geez, Boy, get it together. Here." Gary handed him a handkerchief. "I didn't suit you up to look like a hack."

Boy took the handkerchief and wiped his face. "I spent years avoiding the law, and now you drag me into its belly."

"This isn't the abode of Johnny Law. This is corrupt, rich, fat-cat land. And we're the mice that are going to help ourselves to the cheese. So, stay cool."

"What?"

"Just relax."

The pair walked down the hall and into a large waiting area. It was empty, aside from a few chairs and a vid streamer on the wall.

"Now, where?" Boy asked.

"Now we wait," Gary replied. He dropped his voice and leaned into Boy's ear. "This is a psychological ploy."

Boy went to sit down.

Gary grabbed his shoulder and stopped him. "Not yet."

The two stood quietly for nearly thirty minutes before a nondescript man in a poorly-fitting suit came to fetch them.

"Please come with me," he said.

Gary Legal and Boy followed, Legal strutting, Boy stiffly trudging along. They were shown to a barren conference room. The walls were blank and painted the Hungarian Passport Office green. The conference table looked like a repurposed high school lunch table. Legal and Boy took a seat at one end while two other men sat on the opposite side. The men were both well-dressed; however, one was not very well-groomed. His hair was disheveled. He needed a shave, and his eyes were bloodshot. In fact, he looked like he had not slept in several days.

"You wanted a consultation," Legal said, "because you know my charges increase when I have to make house calls."

"I thought you were the lawyer for the little guy," the disheveled man said. "No hidden charges, no special rates."

"Are you the little guy?" Legal asked.

"No," the other man said. "We are not. We all know where we stand, so you can cut the posturing. Let's drop the bullshit and get to the bones of this problem."

"And what exactly is that problem?" Legal asked.

"Aliens," the disheveled man said.

"Technology," the other man said. "Alien technology."

"Okay," Legal responded. "And what does that have to do with us?"

"We need to get the technology," the other guy said. "We need to litigate for it."

"Whoa, whoa, whoa, whoa." Legal stood up and put his hands up. "Let me get this straight. You want us to sue aliens to get their technology. Aren't you worried about bad blood?"

"They don't like us anyway," the disheveled man replied. "And we've tried everything else."

"We don't even know your names. Hell, we don't even know if this is a legitimate government operation."

"Technically, it is not," the other guy said. "It's off the books."

"So, if something goes wrong, we'll be hung out to dry." Gary turned to Boy. "Come on, we're out of here. No case is worth this crap."

"Wait," the disheveled man said. "I'm Bob, and this is Oscar. We don't plan to hang you out to dry. You're our only hope."

"Okay, princess, what guarantees can you provide us? And don't start with the money thing because you already know that's a dead argument."

"No," Oscar said. "We know you're a man of...integrity?" Oscar looked at Bob, who shrugged.

"Frankly, we know little about you, except that you win, you're not in it for the coin, and you maintained your silence on the A.I. case—which could have been a disaster for the government and a huge boon for you if it leaked out. And you win. Wait, I said that one already."

"You did, and I do win," Legal replied.

"What does this have to do with my uncle's case?" Boy asked.

"They like that I can keep my mouth shut," Gary explained. "They need this handled quietly."

"Exactly," Oscar agreed. "We need someone who can do the job and not use it as a career move. You have proven that you can be trusted to do that."

"Okay," Legal replied. "So, I ask again, what guarantees can you give us that we will remain safe?"

"You are in no physical danger," Bob explained. "The Ilxtani are not violent in the least."

"So why haven't you people just grabbed the junk?" Boy asked. "That is what you normally do, right?"

"That's exactly what they normally do," Gary said. "That is an excellent point, Boy."

"They are still bigger than us," Bob admitted. "Unfortunately, in the grand scheme of things, we are pretty puny."

"Puny, as in diminutive?" Legal asked. "You're saying the human race is tiny compared to the rest of the universe? Exactly how many species have we met?"

"Apart from your friend Yrgohlon and a few aquatic species out there?" Bob sighed. "Three others. They pass through every so often on their way elsewhere. They've all been at least double our size."

"What about the Ilties?" Boy asked.

"On average, the Ilxtani are about five meters tall," Oscar explained. "And every one of them strives for a perfect balance of body and mind."

"So if they were provoked," Legal said, "they could hand us our asses."

"But they are reasonable and open to discourse and debate," Bob replied.

"So they won't beat us down for talking," Boy stated.

"Precisely," Bob agreed. "And your boss can certainly talk."

"So, is this to be some kind of arbitration?" Legal asked.

"That's the plan." Oscar pulled out a tab. The screen was full of documents and photographs. "This is everything we have on them and our interactions with them. See if you can find a kink."

Legal took the tab and stared off into space. "If I take this case, I'll have to do some traveling."

"Yes," Oscar replied. "The trip should take a few days, maybe a week. They are close by."

"I'll need to study this. What about my current cases?"

"We can work something out," Oscar said. "We have some connections."

"I don't like to cheat."

"It's not cheating," Oscar said. "It's more like cooperating for the greater good. We let a few cases win, lighten your caseload, and you get us some tech."

"Still feels like cheating, but okay. My clients come first."

"Your clients will be well provided for," Oscar assured Legal.

"When would you be ready to leave?" Bob asked.

"I have to wrap up a few things. Maybe a week, maybe two?"

"How about tomorrow?" Oscar asked.

Legal shrugged. "Okay, tomorrow."

"What about Uncle Al?" Boy asked.

"We can invite him along. He can help out."

"You know he'll say no. And nobody will be here to keep an eye on him."

"He's a grown-up. He can take care of himself. He'll be okay," Gary said. "Right, Oscar?"

Oscar nodded. "Nothing will happen to the A.I., as already promised."

Gary patted Boy on the chest. "See, it will be okay. I have all kinds of legal protections set up to keep him safe and sound."

Boy nodded. "Okay."

The remainder of Gary Legal and Boy's day was filled with packing and making arrangements. Legal called all his clients to assure them that their cases would be dealt with in his absence. Boy made sure his house was in order and packed up his necessities. After saying their goodbyes to family and friends, the pair made their way to the spaceport.

A small transport was waiting. It was loaded with amenities and comforts. Boy put on his ears, settled in on a very cushy sofa and sipped on a fruity drink. Gary sat across from him, studying the materials.

"I don't understand," Gary said. "These people seem extremely reasonable and logical. Everything they have done and said suggests that they should be helping us, yet they refuse to even give us even the slightest tech. No medical aid. No environmental assistance. It's not even a harmless entertainment device. Why are they holding out?"

Boy shut off his dump and shrugged. "Maybe it's what they said. They just don't like us."

"That," Gary shook his index finger in Boy's direction. "I could believe that. People can be pretty unlikeable."

"Especially government people," Boy added.

"Exactly," Gary said.

"I don't understand something."

"Just one thing?"

Boy sneered at Gary.

"Sorry," Gary said. "It was there. What are you confused about?"

"You said we were going to 'help ourselves to the cheese,' but you didn't ask for any coin. You hardly ever even talk about the coin. How do you stay in business?"

"Ah." Gary grinned. "That, my friend, is because the universe granted me the gift of being a trustafarian."

"Wait, you're coin-maxed?"

"I am," Gary replied. "My father was a very prominent judge and then a successful politician. He was also a colossal douchebag. But I played by his rules for years. I kissed ass where ass was to be kissed. I played ball, scratched the other guy's back, all that jazz."

"When my father was satisfied that I would carry on his corrupt, fat-cat tradition, he gave me his living inheritance. Then I became the biggest pain in his ass I could be. I volunteered at every bleeding-heart liberal law center I could find. I fought every anti-establishment cause that I could join."

"I defended every downtrodden, disenfranchised, unrepresented clod out there. I was a complete embarrassment to him. Holidays were particularly awkward. But I was determined to stay the course. The more he suffered, the happier and more dedicated I became."

"Then, one day, he called to make his peace with me. He said that he accepted me as I was and that he was proud. My whole reason for fighting was gone."

"Why do you still do it?" Boy asked.

Gary shrugged. "It's who I am. I spent months pondering how to move forward with my life. What did I want to do next? And at the end of the day, I realized that I liked it. It wasn't just about pissing my father off. I drank the Kool-Aid. I believed. So, if this thing is going to help people, I'm committed. I will help humanity if humanity can be helped."

Boy nodded. "A lot of stuff makes more sense now."

"Yeah? Well, it's your turn now. Why did you decide to work for me? You had a promising future as an engineer."

"I didn't like it that much, but I didn't want to tell G-pop. He was so happy that I was following in his footsteps. So, I did it for him. After he died, my heart wasn't in it at all. I knew enough to help Uncle Al, and that's all that mattered."

"So, we were on opposite sides of the coin."

"Yeah, I guess we were."

"Why the law?" Gary asked.

"Every time I went to your office, it felt real, and for some reason, I wanted to be there. So, I applied. Then you hired me."

"And I'm glad to have you." Gary smiled. "You have any thoughts on the case?"

"Yeah," Boy said. "They're aliens. We have no idea what they think or how. The only other alien we met was a dev wannabe, and he was obsessed with his comm service."

"True," Gary said. "But these aliens demonstrate behaviors that denote a pattern of reason. Given our previous experience, I find it hard to believe that any race can be so random that we have no common ground. Even the worst of these bureaucrats should have made some headway with them."

"Look who you're talking about," Boy pointed out. "Our government is not always reasonable itself."

"True, but *every* representative they sent?"

"Never underestimate stupidity," Boy replied.

"Wow, you may be even more anti-establishment than me, my friend."

"Why wouldn't I be?" Boy asked.

"Why not, indeed." Gary laughed and shook his head.

The trip to the Ilxtani diplomatic vessel took six hours. It was parked just outside of the Moon's orbit. Gary and Boy freshened up in preparation for their meeting.

The Earth ship docked with the Ilxtani vessel without issue. Gary Legal and Boy, alone, stepped aboard to an empty hallway. There was only one direction to walk.

"Very homey," Gary commented. "Nice."

The ship was lit like a suburban living room. The colors of the walls and floors were warm and inviting, not the cool, industrial hues of Terran space vessels. The outer walls were lined with windows from floor to ceiling. From this angle, they provided a stunning view of the Earth and a corner of the Moon. Gary paused for a moment and enjoyed the view. Boy stepped up next to him.

"Wow," Boy's eyes widened, and his jaw dropped in awe.

"Exactly," Gary replied.

"I only left the Earth once before," Boy said. "And this is a lot better than the Maruti."

"There's a second time for everything." Gary tilted his head toward the gigantic expanse of the hallway. "Come on. Let's see what lies ahead."

292

Boy and Gary walked down the hall to the end, where they were greeted by a massive six-meter-high door. It had no handle or button. It was a blank sheet of copper-colored metal that appeared to slide within the frame.

Boy took the initiative and knocked on the door.

It opened.

Gary nodded in approval.

Another large hallway greeted them. This one had lights along the floor, which seemed to indicate the route to their destination.

"I guess we go that way." Gary pointed at the lights.

They walked until they were standing before another door. It was as massive as the last door and appeared to be an entrance to a room. The door opened, revealing a large conference room. The furniture was humongous. The people seated around the table matched it in stature. Gary Legal and Boy looked like toys compared to them.

A massive hand motioned to a pair of chairs that were obviously modified and had the look of children's booster seats. Gary, for once, was happy with his years of gym attendance. He climbed into the chair with ease. Boy, on the other hand, struggled. One of the meeting's hosts snickered from across the table.

Once they were seated, the pair peered up over the table. The view was daunting. Four humanoid aliens were seated around the table. Physically, they appeared very similar to human beings, the predominant difference being their size. To a human eye, two appeared to be male and two were females. The smallest of the group was one of the female-looking aliens, and she was four meters tall. Gary had to lean over and smack Boy, who was very obviously staring at her.

"Sorry," Boy apologized. "She's very pretty."

The woman obviously heard Boy because she blushed.

"Way to go, cowboy. Try not to get us into an alien harassment suit."

"Oops."

"We're not sure why you're here," the other female host said. She spoke softly, but her voice still boomed. "We already told your government that we'll give you nothing."

"Ma'am, we mean no disrespect," Legal said. "My government asked me to come speak to you one last time, just to see if there was any deal I could broker. I have no knowledge of what occurred in the previous negotiations, but I suspect it was handled with the same

294

diplomacy and flair my government's fine bureaucracy is known for. So, they sent me, a regular guy, to speak to you as a kind voice of the people. Maybe I can appeal to your mercy and compassion."

"Your government wants to take technology it does not have the maturity to handle," the largest male participant said. "You want weapons and transportation technology. Why would we want to put these things in our hands? So, you could come and bring war to the universe?"

"That," Legal responded, "is a good point. But we don't need weapons. Surely there are other technologies you can give us. For example, energy."

"That can be weaponized," the other male participant objected. "Energy technology is not an option."

"How about food production?" Legal asked.

"That uses some of the technologies that could be weaponized." The woman spoke again.

"Okay, maybe some medical technology. It doesn't have to be your cutting-edge stuff, just a nudge in the right direction, something to help our quality of life."

"Why would we give you anything?" the large man asked. "There is no advantage in it for us. What possible motivation would we have?"

"People are suffering," Legal replied. "We have needs, needs that your technology could provide for."

"Your people suffer because you do harm to each other," the large man said.

"Not all of it," Legal replied. "Disease and aging are something we do not do to ourselves."

"Yet you fail to devote resources to it," the woman retorted. "You waste your time and efforts on pointless, petty pursuits, like fighting with each other."

"We've been through all of this already," the large man stated. "You have said nothing new."

"Legally speaking, but by doing nothing when you can help someone in distress, you are guilty of negligence."

"Your Earth laws do not apply to us." The man's voice got slightly louder, enough to cause mild discomfort.

Gary winced. Boy covered his ears.

"Dob, your voice," the woman said.

"Sorry, Tora," Dob said. "They aggravate me."

"What are your thoughts, Hapa?" Tora asked.

"I can't help but think back to the Georu," Hapa replied.

"And the Fnut," the yet unnamed male responded.

"The Fnut were unfortunate," Hapa said. "I deeply regret that decision."

"Well," Legal said, "we are not the Fnut or the Georu."

"No," Dob said. "You're worse than both of them combined."

"Your species is a tiny, yapping fleck of annoyance," the unnamed male stated. "I would wish you all dead, but that would take too much effort."

"Tov," Hapa scolded. She turned to Gary Legal. "I apologize, but our previous experiences sharing technology have been unpleasant."

"Unpleasant, how?" Legal asked.

"The Fnut destroyed themselves," Hapa replied. "We weren't even out of their star system before they eradicated all life in their world."

"They only wanted a power source," Tov stated.

"The Georu only wanted space travel," Dob said. "We provided it. Now, they terrorize their local star cluster. They stole technology from every race they encountered and now call themselves an empire. They cruelly rule over many innocent races because of us."

"I know that's bad, but we are not the same. And," Legal persisted, "we are only asking for help. We don't have any desire to rule over anyone or start any trouble."

"They sent the king of liars," Tov said.

"Hey…"

"We have observed your planet for some time," Hapa said. "You are violent and aggressive."

"Not all of us," Boy interjected.

"The ones in charge are," Tora stated.

Boy started tapping his foot on his chair nervously. Gary glared at him and returned to the conversation.

"I got nothing," Legal said. "But it's the little guy who suffers here. Us nonviolent, peaceful, law-abiding folk suffer because of the actions of our politicians."

"You keep electing them," Dob replied.

"What should we do?" Legal asked. "Start a violent uprising? Destroy the planet in protest? It's not an easy problem to solve."

"That is why you are not ready for our technology," Tora said.

"There has got to be some way," Legal pleaded. "We really need the help."

Boy started tapping his foot on his chair leg again. Legal tried to kick him under the table but missed.

"Your people have nothing to offer us, the universe, or even themselves. What—"

Boy's movements powered up his music dump. His headphones blared, and the electronic cacophony of quadsteamwave filled the room. The hypnotic rhythm overtook the meeting, and soon, all participants were rocking in one way or another to the tune. All the participants but Legal, that was.

"Boy!" Legal shouted. "Could you turn that infernal…"

"What is that?" Dob asked.

"It's my music dump," Boy responded.

"Music dump?" Tora inquired.

"Digital Music Player," Legal replied.

"What is that music it is playing?" Hapa asked.

"Progressive quadsteamwave," Boy answered. "It is the evolution of ancient forms of music we call vaporwave and progressive trance."

"We must have it!" Tov demanded.

Legal grinned. "Maybe we can work out some kind of trade."

—\/\/\—

The moment Gary Legal and Boy made it back to their ship, Gary plugged the crystal drive with the data into the ship's computers.

"Let's send this data back home," Gary said, "before they change their minds."

"I think we should wait until we get home," Boy said, "so they can't screw us."

"Good call," Gary said. "Calling Bob and Oscar now."

"Oscar here." Oscar's face appeared on the vid screen.

There was movement among the people behind him. It was not clear how many, however.

"Hey, Gary and Boy here," Gary said. "We're on our way home. We have your data."

"Excellent." Oscar grinned. "My congratulations on your success. Go ahead and transmit the data now."

"Not so fast," Legal replied. "First, we land, and then we turn over the data."

"Sorry, can't do that," Oscar said. "We have strict instructions not to let you land until we have the data."

"How do you plan to stop us?" Boy challenged him.

An explosion rocked the transport from just outside the hull.

"That was a warning shot," Oscar stated. "Just send over the data before they aim for something important."

"You'd risk destroying the data to keep us from landing?" Gary asked.

"We have excellent data recovery experts," Oscar replied. "Besides, the second you plugged your crystal into the ship's computers, it was streamed over to the backup satellites. Bob just wants to take a look-see."

"Are you kidding? Fine." Legal transmitted the data from the crystal drive. "There, stop shooting, and let us land."

"Thank you," Oscar replied. "Got it. How's it look, Bob?"

Bob giggled. "It's like Christmas."

"Great, so we'll just be heading on…"

"What the hell?" Boy yelled. "Why are we going away from Earth?"

"Yeah," Oscar replied. "That."

"Let's hear it," Legal said. "Let me guess, we know too much to let us live."

"No," Oscar replied. "No, upper management just decided that since you were so effective at taking care of this little problem, we're going to keep you out there for a while, you know, to take care of other pesky issues as they pop up."

"Where exactly is 'out there'?" Legal asked.

"The Outer Colonies," Oscar replied. "Just so your departures and returns can't be as easily monitored by the media."

"You bastard!" Boy launched himself at the vid screen.

Gary caught him before he smashed it with his fist. "That wasn't the deal. You made assurances."

"Yeah, things changed," Oscar replied. "Things above my pay grade."

"You know this isn't over." Legal leaned close to the screen. "I have people, too."

Oscar went pale. "Gotta go." The screen went blank.

Boy stood there, stewing in his anger.

"Listen, Boy," Gary said. "You know I'll fix this. I always do."

"You said there would be fat cat cheese."

"I know, I know…"

"There was no cheese!" Boy screamed.

"Sorry, buddy. Sometimes, the cheese is a lie."

THE END

About the Author

Margret A. Treiber is a witty author and IT enthusiast who thrives on chaos and creativity. Her stories weave humor into everyday life, often blurring the line between reality and absurdity. Margret offers a refreshing perspective on the intersection of technology and storytelling, aiming to make you laugh and think simultaneously. Her engaging style is often dark but satirical, sprinkled into speculative shenanigans flavored with the bittersweet trauma of long-term tech support exposure.

Margret A. Treiber guarantees a surprising and captivating read. She's always one click away from being mistaken for a robot.